POUNDED BY THE CLASSICS

Seven Literary Tales Of The Tingleverse

CHUCK TINGLE

Copyright © 2021 Chuck Tingle

All rights reserved.

ISBN: 9798457431362

CONTENTS

1	The Picture Of Dorian Gay	1
2	20,000 Pounds Into My Butt	12
3	Happy Birthday Frankenstein, Now Pound My Butt	23
4	Happy Birthday Dracula, Now Pound My Butt	35
5	I Have No Butt And I Must Pound	46
6	The Great Gatsbutt	59
7	The Tell-Tale Butt	70

THE PICTURE OF DORIAN GAY

The knock on my loft door couldn't come soon enough.

I erupt to my feet and hurry over, swiftly unlocking the bolt and yanking it open. There, standing on the darkened porch is my dear friend Pazel, a confused and slightly alarmed expression plastered across his face.

"Do you have your things?" I question.

Pazel motions down at the bag of art supplies gripped tight in his hand, a large rectangular case containing what I can only assume are oil paints, brushes and a single canvas. "Everything's here, although there is more to crafting great art than the appropriate tools. You need inspiration, too."

"You've never had a problem with that, Pazel," I counter, opening the door a little wider and allowing my friend passage within.

Pazel steps inside curiously, glancing around as though someone might pop out of the shadows and shock him with a wicked prank.

"I've gotta say, I was a little surprised to get your call," my friend continues. "I love painting you, of course, but this late hour is something new."

"I know, I know," I stammer. "I'm sorry."

"And your request is… well… a lot to ask," Pazel continues. "I can't think of many *masterpieces* that were painted on a whim. These things take patience and passion."

I place my hands on my friend's shoulders, looking him directly in the eyes. "Well, I may not have either of those things, but you've got both and plenty left over to share. I know what you're capable of, Pazel. I believe in you."

I hope my speech comes off as inspiring, not desperate, but it's a fine line to walk with this much anxiety bubbling up inside you. Truth be told, I *am* feeling the dull flame of worry as it nips at my toes, threating to ingulf me if I turn my back and leave it to burn, but at least I'm being proactive against this horrifying potential outcome.

Come on, I think to myself. *Would it really be that bad? Are you really that afraid to admit you're…*

I push these thoughts out of my mind, unwilling to approach that potential outcome just yet. I want to stay positive, to give Pazel something to work with as he captures my essence on canvas. When people see this painting they will know, without a doubt in their mind, that I'm straight.

"You sure you want me to do this right now?" Pazel questions. "You're looking a little… pallid."

"Yes, of course," I continue. "It must be tonight."

My friend hesitates. "You know, if you really want me to capture your essence then you'll need to be honest with me. The relationship between artist and subject is an important one, and if you want a masterpiece then it's gonna require full transparency."

I take a deep breath and let it out, still on the fence with how to handle all this but certainly accepting the wisdom of my friend's commentary. He's not wrong.

"I've been having… strange thoughts," I finally admit.

I let this comment linger in the air for a moment, the statement hovering between us and coloring the silence like Pazel might wash a darkening sky with somber indigo.

"Strange?" Pazel continues, almost chuckling at my vague explanation. "What do you mean strange?"

I lower my voice to a whisper, glancing back and forth over my shoulder as though someone might be listening in from the shadows of my own loft. "Gay," I finally admit.

Pazel pauses for a beat, then suddenly erupts in a fit of laughter. He's utterly beside himself, trying desperately to contain his amusement and failing miserably.

"You're worried that you're *gay?*" he questions. "What's wrong with being gay? *I'm* gay!"

I nod, my face flushing with embarrassment. "I know you are, but *I'm not!*" I cry out. "I'm as straight as they come!"

Pazel gives me a long, long look, and I get the sense that his expression is an attempt to deliver a message that words simply cannot. Whatever this message is, however, I don't receive it.

Finally, my friend lets out a long sigh of acceptance. "Okay then, lets see if we can paint you a masterpiece."

Pazel unzips his bag and pulls out his canvas and a foldable wooden easel, setting it up and then carefully laying out his paints. He motions to a nearby chair and instructs me to pull it over.

I move the chair, placing it before Pazel.

"Sit," he commands.

I do as I'm told, positioning myself in front of my friend as he gets to work.

Pazel pushes forth large splotches of colorful paint across his pallet. He gently mixes them together, manifesting the perfect hues to match my complexion. My friend has painted me several times before, and the results are always breathtaking, but never before has he taken this much time to get things absolutely perfect.

"You know, masterpieces are a little different than a normal painting," Pazel eventually informs me. "As an artist, I can bend the truth to fit my vision, but a *masterpiece* doesn't work like that. When I paint you tonight, I'm going to capture your inner truth whether you like it or not."

"That's exactly what I'm looking for," I reply confidently, "because I'm definitely, definitely, *definitely* not gay."

Pazel smiles, hoisting his brush and then diving in. My friend works diligently, his eyes shifting their focus from me to the canvas with potent intensity. His demeanor changes entirely, like some peak performance athlete in the most important game of their career.

I make sure to find a balance between standing still and relaxing the muscles of my face, providing the best subject that I possibly can.

"It's okay," Pazel eventually offers, the words loosely spilling out of his mouth while the rest of his expression remains fully engrossed. "You can relax. I'm painting your soul, not your body."

I'm not entirely sure what this means, but I do my best to heed his words.

The night wears on and on, but not quite as long as I'd expect for a true masterwork. Soon enough, Pazel sits back and gazes at his finished product. He looks back and forth between me and the painting, adding a single brush stroke and then nodding in confirmation.

"Finished," he finally announces. "It's perfect."

I climb to my feet and hurry over to my friend, anxious to see what he's crafted. The second I round the edge of this canvas I'm in complete awe, nearly buckling at the knees at the overwhelming beauty of this portrait.

My depiction sits with poise and honor, a handsome, masculine man who is strong, honorable, and most of all, straight.

"It's perfect," I offer, utterly mesmerized. "Just perfect."

The smell of savory home cooking fills my home with a cozy warmth as I hurry this way and that, making sure things are in order before my guests arrive.

Suddenly, there's a loud knock at the door, the familiar sound making me jump with excitement. I've had plenty of dinner parties, but this one is particularly special.

Tonight is the night that my friends and colleagues get their first look at Pazel's masterpiece.

I hurry to the front door and yank it open, greeting my first arrivals with an eruption of excitement. It's my friends, Todd and Amanda, and I bless each of them with a powerful hug.

"You made it!" I cry out.

"Wouldn't have missed it for the world, Dorian," Amanda replies. "I can't wait to get a look at this new painting you've been raving about."

"Well, the wait is over," I offer with a smirk. "Come on in."

My friends step inside and hang their coats, then continue onward into the den. It's here Pazel's notorious portrait hangs, positioned above my fireplace.

"Right this way!" I continue, leading them forward and then motioning toward the grand painting. "Feast your eyes."

My breath suddenly catches in my throat, shocked by what I see. Technically speaking, the painting is still just as masterful as it's always been, but there are glaring details I hadn't noticed until just now. Yes, I still appear to be *mostly* straight, but up until this point I hadn't realized I was depicted wearing a mesh, see-through shirt.

"It's amazing," Amanda gushes.

"Whoa," Todd chimes in. "Incredible."

I'm frozen in terror, not quite sure how to react. My friends are proceeding as though everything is just fine, but the apparel on display is making me uneasy.

"Yeah… thanks," I stammer, suddenly not as interested in showing off this new work of art. "Let's go take our seats in the kitchen. Dinner's almost ready."

I coax my friends back into the other room, making them aware of a beautiful hors d'oeuvres assortment that's been laid out for snacking. They quickly settle in, enjoying their snacks as another loud knock erupts through my loft.

"Coming!" I call out, leaving Todd and Amanda behind.

I make my way to the front door, opening it up to reveal another old friend, Borson Reems.

"Welcome!" I offer, smiling as I see this stout, bearded man. "Come in, come in."

Borson steps inside, hanging his coat and hat.

"The food is almost ready," I continue. "Let's head to the kitchen."

"Already?" Borson interjects. "Come on, show me the painting!"

I try my best to brush off his request. "Oh that? It's nothing really. Trust me, the *food* will be the star of the show this evening."

Borson laughs and pushes past me. "Oh Dorian, you're such a kidder," he booms. "Now, where is this masterpiece?"

I scramble to follow behind as my friend makes his way into the den. I'm already blushing with embarrassment as I struggle to keep him at bay.

"It's really nothing," I cry out. "Forget I even mentioned it."

It quickly becomes apparent, however, that Borson is on a mission and he will not be deterred. My only hope now is that these imperfections aren't quite as bad as I thought. Maybe the mesh shirt is barely noticeable.

The next thing I know, Borson is standing in my den, gazing up at the portrait in admiration.

"Wow," is all that he can say, his eyes twinkling and his mouth agape with wonder. "This is *beautiful.*"

Unfortunately, my reaction is not quite as positive. Somehow, Pazel's artwork has captured me in an even *gayer* aesthetic than before, a rainbow flag held tight in my hands as I hoist it behind me.

I absolutely *do not* remember that being a part of this composition. I'm utterly mortified.

"Oh shit," I blurt, hurrying over to the portrait and grabbing the frame from either side as I lift it off the wall. "There's a slight mistake. I'll need Pazel to make a correction to this very, very straight painting."

"A mistake?" Borson blurts. "What are you talking about? It's breathtaking!"

"Nope," I stammer. "There's a big mistake. Don't worry about it, though."

I hurry over to a nearby closet, opening the door and roughly tossing my painting inside. I slam the closet shut and lock it tight, breathing a loud sigh of relief.

When I turn back around, Borson Reems is eyeing me peculiarly, his eyebrow raised. "If you say so," he finally offers.

More and more guests filter in as the night continues onward, each one of them begging to see the portrait I'd been raving about for days. Of course, I deny every one of these requests, brushing them away and explaining that my talk of a masterpiece had been greatly exaggerated.

My guests are all confused and concerned by my sudden change of heart regarding this artwork; everyone but Pazel.

Strangely, when the painter arrives he doesn't seem at all concerned that I've tucked away his portrait in a closet. I'm worried that my friend is going to be hurt and insulted, but if anything he's slightly amused.

"Captured more than you wanted to see, did I?" Pazel chuckles.

I shake my head. "Hardly," I counter. "You're a fantastic artist and a dear friend, but this portrait is far from your best work."

Pazel says nothing in return, his response offered in the form of a faint, knowing smile at the corner of his mouth.

As the night continues and the party grows in size, I eventually let go of my worries regarding this mysterious painting. Soon enough I've forgotten it's even there tucked away in the closet, simply enjoying the evening with my friends as I'd originally intended.

This state of ignorant bliss lasts late into the evening, but as folks begin to make their goodbyes I find myself haunted by thoughts of the portrait once more.

When I finally close and lock my door around midnight, Pazel's painting has returned to the forefront of my mind.

I shake my head in frustration, as though this might somehow clear out the haze of anxiety that clouds my brain. It doesn't work, however, and as I begin to pace back and forth in my apartment foyer the tension within me only builds.

In a moment of desperation I decide to talk myself down, speaking the words out loud to give them even more weight.

"You're straight as can be," I assure myself, nodding along to this frantic diatribe. "There isn't a gay bone in your body."

Oddly, this self-affirmation seems to help a little, and soon enough my pacing begins to slow.

"Don't worry," I soothe confidently. "It's just a painting."

Eventually, I march into the bathroom, placing my hands on the counter as I stare at myself in the mirror. I take note of the curves of my face, the color of my eyes and the darkness of my wavy hair. I look like *me*.

"Maybe the painting's not so bad," I tell myself, watching the way my lips move in the reflection. "Maybe I'm over reacting."

With a newfound confidence, I return to the den, gazing upon the closed closet door and approaching it slowly. I reach out and undo the lock, hesitating briefly before pulling it upon with a sharp tug.

Light floods in, revealing Pazel's painting in all of its glory.

A startled yelp escapes my throat as I stumble back, horrified by the visage before me. My hope was that my intial impressions were exaggerated, that I'd found a subtle gayness in the portrait that wasn't actually there.

Unfortunately, the exact opposite is true.

In addition to the mesh, see-through shirt and the rainbow flag wrapped around my body, this painting now features a ball gag fetish toy that hangs from my neck. I'm also wearing a black, rabbit-themed masquerade mask and sporting a lip ring.

"Oh my god!" I shriek, grabbing the painting and marching back into the den where my fireplace continues to roar.

I hoist the canvas above my head, ready to throw it into the fire when suddenly an unexpected voice stops me in my tracks.

"That's no way to treat your inner self," comes a soft, confident tone.

I lower the painting and watch in amazement as it floats out of my hands, hovering in the air before me.

"What is this?" I stammer. "Who are you?"

"I'm *you*," the painting replies. "Dorian Gay."

"We can't both be Dorian," I reply.

"Well, we are," the painting continues. "In fact, you might even say I'm a more honest approximation of ourselves."

I shake my head. "That can't possibly be true," I continue. "I'm not gay."

The painting laughs. "You sure about that? Don't you think it's a little on-the-nose that you tucked me away in your closet?"

"That's... just a coincidence," I counter.

"Oh yeah?" the painting continues, slowly hovering toward me. "How about this?"

He reaches out and places a hand on my chest, running his fingers across me slowly and sending a sharp chill of arousal down my spine.

"Are these feelings a mistake, too?" the portrait coos.

I shake my head, finally admitting something I've known in my heart all along. "No, it's not a mistake," I sigh. "I want you so badly."

Suddenly, the portrait and me are all over one another, our hands caressing each other's bodies with carnal enthusiasm. Our lips meet in a flurry of passionate kisses, completely lost in the moment.

The feeling of this artwork beneath my fingertips is incredible, my digits picking up on every subtle texture of his oil paint construction. He's perfectly crafted, a masterpiece in exactly the way Pazel had said.

I just wasn't ready to see it yet.

Meanwhile, the portrait is having just as much fun exploring *my* body with his roaming hands. He starts at my collarbones and works his was down across my chest, stripping away my shirt in the dancing glow of the fire. When he finally exposes my skin to the warm evening air I let out a soft whimper, completely lost in the moment.

Lower and lower the painting drifts, eventually reaching my waistband. It's here that he teases me for a while, tracing his fingers gracefully across my hips and then finally undoing my belt. Soon enough, he's reaching within and wrapping his hand around my quickly stiffening cock.

"Oh fuck," I groan. "That feels so fucking good."

I begin to grind against the painting as he strokes me in unison, sending waves of incredible pleasure across my body. The pump of my hips quickly falls into sync with the painting's hand, but as the pleasure builds I find myself yearning to switch gears.

This portrait has already given me so much by making me aware of my inner truth, now I want to give something back to him.

Abruptly, I drop to my knees before the artwork, gazing up at him with eyes of ravenous, erotic hunger. Slowly, an enormous shaft begins to emerge from his body, pointing toward my face like a glorious sexual obelisk.

I immediately get to work, licking the painting's cock from base to tip and then playfully kissing the head of his shaft. Next, I open wide and slip his girthy member between my lips, bobbing my head up and down across his length in slow, passionate movements.

"That feels so good," the work of art groans above me, rocking along with the movements of my head.

It's not long before we fall into a rhythm together, the pace steadily quickening as I reach up and play with his hanging balls. I work him like this for a good while until, eventually, the speed is too overwhelming and I pull back with a frantic gasp.

I take a moment to center myself and then open wide yet again, only this time my goal is different. Instead of pumping my face across the painting's cock, I simply allow him to slip deeper and deeper into my gullet. The massive rod plunges well past the expected limits of my gag reflex, plummeting all the way down until he's fully consumed.

My face is now pressed up hard against the oil painting, held in place in a stunning deep throat performance.

I remain like this for as long as I possibly can, savoring the moment of sexual submission and then pulling back with another sloppy gasp.

Now, I'm *really* turned on, and with a fire in my eyes I frantically tear away the rest of my clothing. I turn around and pop my ass out toward the painting, rocking my hips as I seductively crawl away from him. When I reach the couch, I climb up onto it, positioning myself for entry as I reach back and give my ass a playful slap.

"You're not the only masterpiece around here," I offer playfully. "Check out this butthole."

The painting floats down into position behind me, aligning his massive cock with my puckered anal seal. He hesitates for a moment, teasing me with the presence of his giant rod before finally pushing deep in one long, powerful swoop.

"Oh fuck!" I blurt, gripping tight against the fabric before me.

The painting's size is incredible, filling me up completely and stretching my ass to the absolute limits. Fortunately, this handsome piece of artwork is willing to take his time with me, holding tight but refusing to move until my body adjusts to his mammoth member.

Gradually, the discomfort begins to melt away, slowly dissipating as a pleasant fullness and warmth take its place. Soon enough, the two of us are rocking against one another while pleasure floods through me, the living painting's cock pushing gracefully in and out of my tight ass.

I brace myself against the couch, positioning my body for even deeper entry and arching my back in the light of the dancing fire.

"Just like that, just like that," I begin to moan, repeating these words over and over again as the portrait continues to rail away.

I reach down between my legs and grab ahold of my hanging cock, pumping my fist across the length in time with this artwork's powerful thrusts. He knows exactly how to pound me, his cock reaching my absolute depths and causing a pulse of delicious fullness to spill out across my veins.

These two distinct sources of pleasure churn together beautifully, creating something so much more than just the sum of their parts. I'm beside myself with pleasure, my eyes rolling back into my head as my body begins to tremble and quake.

"Harder! Harder!" I scream, my frantic cries filling the apartment as I desperately beg for more.

As the painting slams me like a jackhammer, I find myself consumed by a powerful sensation at the pit of my stomach. The tension floods my veins, looming larger and larger in a tidal wave that's threatening to crest, and although I recognize this feeling as an impending orgasm, there's something else swirling within that I didn't expect.

This release is not just a physical one, but emotional and spiritual, too, an expression of something that lurks at the very core of my being.

As the orgasm grows closer, I find words bubbling up and dancing across my lips, desperate to spill over. "I'm... I'm..." I stammer, the full sentence threatening to break like a powerful sneeze. "I'm... gay!"

The climax hits me hard, surging through my body and sweeping me away in an ocean of freedom and acceptance. Jizz erupts hard from the head of my cock, splattering across the couch below me as I tremble and quake.

Meanwhile, the painting pushes deep and holds, erupting with a payload of his own. He pumps into my body with his oil paint spunk, filling me to the brim and then eventually spurting from the sides of my ass when there's just no room left.

When the portrait finally finishes the two of us collapse into a fucked silly heap, struggling to catch our breath as we bask in a state of utter satisfaction.

"That was incredible," I gush, pulling the portrait close and gazing deep into his eyes.

We stay like this for a while, just enjoying one another's presence. As I continue to take the painting in, I find myself compelled to make an admission.

"I've gotta say, I kind of expected you to revert back to the original look I saw in my head," I offer, "but I guess this is *really me.*"

The masterpiece laughs. "Both of us are *really you,*" he counters. "There's no right or wrong way to be queer. If you want to wear a bunny masquerade mask and dance around with your pride flag in a mesh, see-through shirt, that's great! And if you want to *not* do any of those things, that's great too! You're a perfect version of yourself just the way you are."

I smile, nodding with understanding. "I feel like I need to call my friends and organize another dinner party," I offer, "and this time you're not getting stuffed away in the closet."

20,000 POUNDS INTO MY BUTT

Sitting in my chambers and gazing out through this massive, round window, I can't help allowing the frustration to wash over me. I know I should maintain a sense of gratitude at a moment like this, taking solace in what I *have* instead of submitting to what I desire, but this honorable philosophy has grown difficult to maintain.

    I try my best to hold an air of calm, collected strength as I guide my crew, a fearless leader to look up to and emulate. Right now, however, the veil has slipped in the dim light of my cabin.

    I'm exhausted and deeply troubled, not even the sight of these glorious undersea landscapes providing the rush of excitement they once did.

    I gaze out through the viewing window, watching as various tiny fishes and an assortment of colorful seaweed passes me by. The vista is breathtaking, an assortment of hills and valleys that cascade on and on across the ocean floor, but the wonder of this uncharted land leaves me unphased.

    A year ago, I might stand before this massive glass pane and feel energized by these sights, blown away by the fact that no other human eye had gazed upon the ridges, but those days are long gone.

    A soft knock on the chamber door washes across my ears, but I do not rise from my bench. I think to react, but the sadness that overwhelms my body holds me at bay. My mind is well aware I should move, but my body doesn't quite have the energy to make this happen.

    The knock comes once again, a little louder this time.

    "Captain Neno?" drifts a voice from behind the thick metal wall, barely audible. "Is everything alright in there?"

I let out a loud sigh, finally realizing that I'll have to speak up at some point. I don't want my friend to worry, after all.

"Yes Consal!" I call out. "I'm fine."

There's a moment of hesitation. "Can I come in?"

"Fine," I groan, refusing to stand but granting him entry.

There's a loud clang as the door opens behind me, my loyal first mate and dear friend entering slowly. I don't turn around to greet him, just keep my eyes transfixed on the underwater vista beyond.

Consal sits on the bench next to me, silently watching this glorious landscape pass. Just being in his presence sets me at ease, the hardened edge of my personality softening ever so slightly. He's the one crew member any with emotional sway over me, but I suppose that comes with the territory when you've known each other for this long.

"Storm's brewing," my friend finally offers.

My eyes flicker upward curiously. "We won't need to surface for several days," I retort. "What good will any news of the weather do me?"

Consal places a hand on my shoulder, heaping on unspoken love and affection through this simple gesture. "I wasn't talking about the surface, I was talking about a storm in your heart."

I laugh, amused by my friend's poetic flair. In a situation like this, he's the only one who can pull me out of the darkness, if only for a brief moment.

"I'm sorry," I finally reply. "I want to maintain a confident outlook for the rest of the crew, but you're right to sense some doubt in me. I'm worried this undersea world might prove just as disappointing as the land above."

I can tell Consal is a little shocked to hear me say this, reeling from my admission as he struggles to push onward with words of encouragement. Looks like he didn't quite know what he was getting into when he came down here to talk some sense into me.

"There's still plenty of unexplored ocean left," my first mate finally replies. "You'll find a twenty thousandth pound soon enough."

He's assertive in his reminder, but it only serves to make me think of the last time I was privy to this kind of oath.

Long, long ago, I was a simple surface dweller just like the rest of them, living my life in the sun and experiencing all the great wide world had to offer. Like most folks, I enjoyed a good pound in the butt every now and then, and in my journeys I encountered all kinds of partners for this glorious carnal act of love.

I took them all in bed; dinosaurs, bigfeet, unicorns and living objects, and as my number of illicit experiences began to grow, I found myself yearning for more. I would travel around the globe to enjoy my anal pounds, an epicure on a mission to experience every kind of butt slamming imaginable.

I decided upon a goal, a nice round number that could easily communicate the vast scale of this erotic quest. After going back and forth for a while, I finally decided twenty thousand pounds was the perfect amount.

The beginning of my journey was an absolute blast, cocks in my butt and a song in my heart as I traveled globe in search of unique and exciting encounters. In those days, it seemed like a new pound was waiting around every corner, just begging to sweep you away on the adventure of a lifetime at a moment's notice.

As time rolled on, however, unique sexual experiences became few and far between. I'm quite handsome, but that's not all there is to an erotic connection.

Eventually, I'd ran through every species of land-dwelling dinosaur and every brilliant breed of sparkling unicorn. I pounded my way through each living object I could find, my sexual history looking more like a dictionary than a list of partners.

I barely made it to ten thousand pounds, halfway to my goal and no chance in hell I'd actually make it.

People tried to be encouraging, telling me ten thousand pounds was still an incredible accomplishment, and I suppose they're right. Still, it wasn't the goal I set out to hit.

I remember feeling despondent at that time, utterly devastated by the realization that I'd never receive twenty thousand anal slams no matter how hard I tried. It started to eat away at me, driving me further and further into a state of isolation and darkness.

That's when the moment of great inspiration came, the idea that would change my life forever. While the surface of our planet holds a wide variety of potential pounds, there's *many more* unique partners to be found below the ocean. If I wanted to reach my goal I'd have to start on an entirely new landscape.

Thus, I got to work constructing my vessel, a submarine affectionately known as the *Buttalis*. With this incredible machine I've been able to escape the confines of the world above, continuing my twenty thousand pound journey far away from the world that had so deeply disappointed me all those years ago.

"I appreciate your vote of confidence," I offer Consal, "but I'm beginning to worry this mission is headed toward the same fate as my last."

My first mate shakes his head. "Don't say that, Neno. We're so close."

He's correct in this assertation. After all this time, I've found myself balancing upon the precipice of my own self-imposed finish line, nineteen thousand nine hundred and ninety nine pounds to my name. My butt has taken then all, and I've thoroughly enjoyed every step of this journey.

Truth be told, it's been more and more difficult to find the next exciting anal slam with every passing day, and the last few were damn near impossible despite our deep explorations of the Mariana Trench.

Now, with only one pound left in my epic journey, we've come to a standstill.

The very idea of a fully charted ocean floor is absurd, but here we are with two months behind us and not a single unique encounter.

"There's one more pound out there," Consal assures me. "Even if there's not, we've gotta keep searching."

I take a deep breath and let it out, struggling to let his kind words of assurance seep through the hard shell around my soul

My first mate is right about one thing, regardless of a final pound's likelihood, our mission is more than just a specific number. We're explorers to the core, wanderers who push onward into the unknown no matter what happens.

I may have briefly forgotten this powerful truth, but no longer.

"You're right," I retort, rising to my feet and strolling closer to the round viewing window. I gaze out at the glorious submerged vista before us, pushing away any negative thoughts and appreciating it for the wonderous landscape that it is. "The search is not over yet."

I can see my first mate in the reflection of this window, a smile creeping its way across his face.

"The spark of exploration is never finished!" I suddenly bellow, my voice carrying out through the submarine with deafening confidence. I point to a set of cavernous tunnels on the starboard side. "There! Set a course! Let's see if we can find anything new to pound my butt!"

"Aye aye, Captain!" Consal retorts, jumping to his feet with a firm salute and then hurrying off.

I stay back a little while longer, watching as the *Buttalis* creeps closer and closer to the darkness of these strange a mysterious caverns.

Eventually, I head to the captain's bridge. It's here than I can get a report on our entire vessel and make any calls about what to do next.

By the time I arrive at the bridge, our vessel has entered the caverns and this room is already buzzing with excitement. One of our engineers swiftly approaches me.

"Captain Neno," he begins, overflowing with excitement. "This cave is very unusual. The temperature of the water is well below what you might expect for the area, leading me to believe that we might've stumbled across an opening into an even deeper trench."

"A deeper trench you say?" I reply, the twinkle of adventure in my eye. "How deep?"

"There's no telling," my engineer continues. "However, the cold shift makes me believe this opening could've occurred very recently. We're likely drifting into prehistoric waters."

"Let's light up the front beam and see what we've got!" I call out.

The bridge crew immediately gets to work, hustling and bustling from one station to the next as they prepare our front facing observation deck. This window is smaller than the one in my personal quarters, but it's equipped with a powerful tool.

The *Buttalis* only has so much energy to draw from, so we can't use the front facing light often, but these particularly dark caverns are exactly the place for it. This incredibly powerful beam that will illuminate a concentrated area as though it were daylight.

My heart pounding within my chest, I glance over at my first mate Consal. For a brief moment I thought I'd never feel this kind of excitement again, and all it took was a few kind words from my friend to pull me back from the edge.

Everyone feels down sometimes, but it's important to reach out because you never know what might be waiting just around the corner.

"Is the beam ready?" I call out.

"Ready, sir!" replies Consal.

"Light it up!" I continue.

Suddenly, the viewing window erupts in a bloom of glorious illumination, the beam so brilliant that I'm momentarily forced to shield my eyes before gradually settling in. When I finally gaze out at the ocean beyond I catch sight of something in the haze, a tentacle just barely slinking off into the shadows.

"There!" I yell out. "Is that what I think it is?"

"I don't see anything, Captain," Consal interjects.

"Bring me voice controls," I continue.

A crew member hurries over and hands me a microphone, allowing my words to radiate out into the water around us.

I clear my throat, and click the button of this auditory announcement system. "Excuse me," I begin. "I'm very sorry for barging into your caverns. This is Captain Neno of the *Buttalis,* and I'm looking for unique and handsome lifeforms to pound my ass. Is anyone out there?"

The crew waits in silence, gazing out into the ocean with baited breath.

"I could've sworn I saw a tentacle," I continue. "If there's a handsome kraken out there, I would *love* for you to pound me in the butt."

Very slowly, a figure begins to emerge from the shadows and into my ship's brilliant illumination.

I gasp when I see him, a handsome, muscular man with the head of a squid and the chiseled body of Neptune.

"Oh my god," I gasp, overwhelmed with arousal as I lay eyes on this incredible creature. "The kraken."

"If you're interested in meeting up and seeing how we vibe, there's a hatch on top of the ship," I continue into the microphone. "Do you breathe air as well as water?"

The kraken nods.

"I'll meet you up there," I continue.

I shut off the microphone and my crew erupts with furious applause, hooting and hollering over the first potential pound in months. Of course, this is more than just another sexual encounter after an epic dry spell, this could be the twenty thousandth pound we've been looking for, the end to this epic quest they all said could never be accomplished.

"Now, now," I continue, quieting down the crew. "Who knows what could happen. We might not get along. Don't get your hopes up just yet."

I'm trying to keep their expectations in check, but even I can't help the spring in my step as I leave the bridge and head up to the airlock.

When I arrive, the handsome kraken is already inside, this mysterious prehistoric creature patiently waiting in silence. I glance through the eyehole, taking in his incredibly toned body, then open the metal door that separates us.

"Be cool, be cool," I keep repeating under my breath, struggling to remain calm.

You'd think after all this time I'd be used to these first steps of courtship, but even after nineteen thousand nine hundred and ninety nine pounds I still get butterflies in my stomach.

When I finally get up the courage I open the metal door that separates us, the hatch swinging wide with a loud creek the emanates through the ship. There standing before me is the handsome kraken, his features even more striking up close.

Typically, I know exactly how to play these situations, but in this particular moment I find myself at a loss for words. The pressure is just too much, and it has fried the circuits that keep me socially affable.

Fortunately, the kraken takes the lead. "Nice ship," he offers. "What's your name?"

"Captain Neno," I stammer, struggling to keep my cool.

"That's what I thought," the prehistoric creature continues. "You're the guy who's going around trying to get pounded by twenty thousand different things under the sea, right?"

I nod.

"How far along are you?" he continues.

"Pretty far," I reply. "Just one left."

The kraken breaks into a smile, clearly impressed. "Damn. That's a hell of a journey. What did you learn? Did you fall in love?"

I consider his words and then shake my head. "There's plenty of stories and anecdotes about about finding love after taking the right pound and it changing your life forever. That's great, honestly. Those stories are very important, and I would never say anything to disparage that."

"But?" the kraken questions, well aware that a shift is coming.

"But... that doesn't have to be *every* story. Having sex doesn't have to offer you some new elevated worldview or help you find the perfect life partner. It doesn't need to alter the timeline that swirls around you or prove love is real in some grand cosmic sense. Sometimes having sex is just about *having fun,* and that's okay, too."

"Ironically, that still proves love is real," the kraken interjects.

"Huh?" I blurt, not quite hearing him.

"What?" the prehistoric sea creature retorts.

We stand awkwardly for a moment until the blossoming arousal finally overtakes any lingering self-consciousness. The next thing I know, me and the muscular sea creature are rushing toward one another and kissing passionately, completely losing ourselves in the moment.

The kraken's writhing tentacles work their way around my face, slipping up and over the top of my head and down around my shoulders in a twisted mass. I feel overwhelmed by their presence, held tight by this cascade of powerful facial appendages.

"Oh fuck," I gush. "That tickles, but in a good way."

It's tough for me to pull away from this wonderful sensation, but I'm on a mission and my focus is laser sharp. Gradually, I slip down across the prehistoric sea creature's body, working my way over his muscular chest in a series of kisses and then dropping to his toned abs. I drift lower and lower across his body, kneeling before him as I gaze up with a look of lustful anticipation.

I unbuckle the kraken's belt, slipping down his soaking wet pants and allowing his giant rod to spring forth. The creature's cock is utterly enormous, projecting out toward my face in a glorious display that literally causes me to gasp in awe.

I glance back up at the kraken, impressed by his size and offering a playful wink.

Wrapping my fingers around his substantial girth, I begin pumping my hand up and down his length a few times just to warm him up. The kraken rocks his body against mine, clearly enjoying this sensation as the two of us fall into sync with one another.

As soon as I understand the temperament of this erotic pulse, I spring into action. Opening wide, I take the kraken's giant rod between my lips, keeping pace with the established momentum.

The kraken moans loudly as I continue to suck him off, his head tilted back and his tentacles squirming with absolute pleasure. The muscular sea creature reaches down and places his hands on the back of my head, taking control of the moment and guiding me gracefully along his swollen member.

Our pace begins to quicken, moving faster and faster until I pull back with a frantic gasp. I take a moment to collect myself, even more belligerent with lust now, then dive back in again.

This time however, I change my technique entirely. Instead of bobbing my head rapidly across the kraken's length, I simply allow him to slide deeper and deeper into my gullet. The prehistoric sea creature's dick slips all the way down, well past the expected limits of my gag reflex and coming to rest at the absolute depths of my throat.

Soon enough, my face is pressed up hard against the kraken's chiseled abs, held tight in a stunning deep throat performance.

I stay like this for as long as I possibly can, allowing the kraken to enjoy his position of power above me and then finally pulling away when I just can't take it anymore. It's not the lack of air that ends this oral maneuver, however.

I need more.

"Fuck me with that giant sea monster cock," I snarl, tearing away my clothing and tossing it to the side. The only thing that remains now is the captain's hat perched atop my head, which somehow makes the rest of my body appear even more nude.

I crawl away from the kraken, wiggling my rump from side to side as he watches me go. I reach back and give my ass a playful slap, teasing him with the sight of my tightly puckered hole.

"What are you waiting for?" I coo. "I'm ready for my twenty thousandth pound."

The prehistoric sea creature climbs down into position behind me, placing the head of his enormous rod at the entrance of my anal seal. I can feel him tease me for a moment, testing my entrance with his mammoth rod and then finally pushing forward with a deep, singular thrust.

A startled yelp escapes my throat, not entirely prepared for the enormity of his member. Taking the kraken's cock between my lips had been one thing, but my asshole is another story entirely. I'm completely filled to the brim, stretched to my limits by this enormous member as my fingers dig hard against the airlock floor below me.

"Oh fuck," I groan, my eyes rolling back into my head. "That sea monster dick feels like it's about to split me in two."

Fortunately, the kraken is a patient lover and is happy to take his time with me. Instead of immediately getting to work, the muscular creature holds tight in the depths of my butthole, allowing any discomfort to slowly melt away. Soon enough, the ache has transformed into a pleasant warmth at the pit of my stomach as my muscles relax.

The kraken begins to pump in and out of me slowly, rocking his hips gently against my body as the two of us fall into rhythm.

"Just like that," I offer encouragingly, egging him on. "Just like that!"

We gradually begin to grind with more and more intensity, the speed building until, eventually, we find ourselves sharing a confident anal pound. Every slam against my backside sends a powerful surge of pleasure through my body, flooding my veins with erotic ache.

I can feel the first hints of a powerful orgasm blossoming in the pit of my stomach, these surges causing my body to tremble and quake as they continue to build. With one hand I reach down and wrap my fingers around my hanging cock, beating myself off in time with the hammering beat of this handsome kraken's anal slams.

"Don't. Stop. Fucking. Me. With. That. Fat. Sea. Monster. Dick," I cry out, each word separated by a singular deep thrust into my shaking body.

There's so much sensation within my frame that I feel as though I'm about to explode, the crackling erotic energy left with nowhere else to go as it struggles to escape my physical form. The tension builds, looming higher and higher like some massive tidal wave and then finally crashing down in a mighty orgasm.

I throw my head back and let out an unbridled shriek, the culmination of more than just this erotic encounter, but several exhausting years of aquatic exploration. This moment is utterly cathartic, the ending to a quest that most said would never be possible.

Hot white jizz erupts from the head of my cock, splattering across the floor below me in a glorious pattern of pearly spunk.

Meanwhile, the kraken diligently carries me through my entire orgasm, never letting up for a second as the sensation completely overwhelms my body. When the climax has finally passed, my sea monster lover plunges deep into my butthole and unleashes a payload of his own.

I can feel the kraken's seed spilling into me, filling my asshole to the brim and then squirting out from the edges when there's simply not enough room left. The cum runs down the back of my leg in several glorious streaks.

The two of us collapse into a satisfied pile. We bask in this moment for a good while, then I finally stand up and begin pulling back on my clothes.

"That was amazing," the kraken offers. "I had a great time."

"Me too," I reply.

There are versions of this moment where the two of us pledge to see each other again or ask what we're doing next week. We could easily fall in love, get married and start a family together if that's what the fates had in store. After all, the chemistry between me in this prehistoric sea monster is palpable.

But not every story has to end with the promise of a future, or a confession of true love, or a ring. It's okay to have a little fun sometimes, to set out on an adventure with no strings attached and follow that path to its conclusion.

Sex is fun, after all, and sometimes it doesn't need to be any more than that.

Sometimes there's nothing wrong with two ships passing in the night.

HAPPY BIRTHDAY FRANKENSTEIN, NOW POUND MY BUTT

Backpacking across Europe is something that most American guys find themselves at least *considering* once we finish college; the open road, nothing to tie us down. After years of tests and textbooks, there's not much that sounds better than that.

I've been on board with this idea since I can remember, planning out all of the stops that I would make along the way. However, while plenty of guys get a group of friends together for this type of adventure, there's something about the idea finding myself on a solo journey that really appeals to me in a big way.

Of course, I quickly found myself running into the same problem that everyone seems to face when they start to consider any sort of undertaking like this; money.

My family is not dirt poor by any means, but we certainly live a modest life out here in Iowa, farming corn and working as hard as we can to make ends meet. I never once complained though, and I learned to appreciate the hardships for the way that they've shaped me. I'd like to think that my demeanor is collected, disciplined and patient from learning the ways of the crops, while my body has been toned to muscular perfection from the yearly harvest.

Still, neither of those things help me pull together enough money to get across Europe on a reasonable budget. With the sum of my modest savings, I could just barely afford the flight there and back, which leaves a whole lot of questions as to where I'll be staying.

Of course, that's kind of the nature of backpacking, the adventure of never knowing where you're going to turn up next. However, without any emergency funds or a little cash to actually enjoy myself once I got over there, my trip was dead in the water.

That is, until the night that my dad sat me down and told me all about our long time family friend, Frankenstein.

I was standing in the kitchen, doing the dishes as I routinely do after my mom makes a delicious home cooked mean, when my dad enters and has a seat at the table behind me.

"Why don't you take a break on those and come over here to talk to your old dad," my father suggests.

As crazy as it may sound, it's honestly quite hard to keep myself from obsessing over doing chores around the house, to the point that it's a struggle putting down the dishes before I'm finished. Maybe I'm being weird about it, but as a full-grown adult ready to enter the world, I feel kind of weird about still living here at home. If I'm going to be in this house, I need to be helping out and proving my worth.

"Just let me finish up here," I call back over my shoulder.

"Come on now, sit down," my dad insists, "there's something I need to talk to you about."

Finally relenting, I turn off the sink and walk over to the table, noting the gravely intense look on my dads face.

"What's up," I ask, taking a seat.

"Your mother and I have been talking," my father begins. "We know how much this trip means to you, you've been planning it for so long and the thought that you won't go just because you can't quite afford it right now is too much for us to bear."

I immediately raise up my hand, stopping my dad immediately. "Listen, before you go any further I am going to tell you that the answer is no. I know how tight money is on the farm, and I'm not going to let you pay for my trip," I tell him. "It's not right."

"No, no, no," says my father with a smile, waving his hand as though it could dissipate the very suggestion as it floats between us. "I admire your class, son, but that's not it at all."

Suddenly, my interest in piqued. Could my father have somehow figured out a way to make this trip a possibility? My mind is already racing with all of the situations that could be at hand, and none of them make any sense at all.

"Have I ever told you about our old family friend, Mr. Frankenstein?" my father asks, a strange glimmer of reverence in his eye. "He was my old college roommate, a science major who built the very first artificial life form."

"Wait, what?" I say, stunned as I reel from this revelation. "What do you mean?" I ask.

"He dug up a bunch of graves and sewed the parts together," my father informs me, "built himself a real life monster and then electrocuted it with a generator. The thing just came to life."

"That's incredible," I gush.

My father leans back into his chair, recalling a part of his life that he clearly hasn't considered in a while. "We were wild back then," he informs me, "Me, Frankie and his creation. It's sad really, because Frankie died not too long after. I stayed in touch with the monster though, through postcards and that kind of thing. He forwards me emails sometimes."

"I'm sorry," I say, shaking my head, "but how is this going to help me get over to Europe?"

"Well, Frankie lives in Germany," explains my father.

"I thought he died," I counter.

My dad laughs. "Oh yeah, sorry about that," he explains jovially. "Eventually, people just started calling the creature Frankie, too, don't ask me why."

"Seems a little morbid," I offer.

"I think he likes it," my father says with a shrug, "probably reminds him of the good ol' days. Anyway, Frankie is in Germany. I've already reached out to him and he would love to have you stay in his penthouse for a week."

"What?" I ask, astonished. "Really?"

My father nods. "It's not a trip across Europe, but at least you'll get to see Berlin. Frankie will let you stay for free, not like he needs the money anyway."

"He's rich?" I ask.

My dad nods. "He's a very famous racecar driver, actually."

"This is the best news I've ever heard!" I shout, jumping up from the table and running around to the other side as I throw my hands around my father.

My dad laughs, clearly pleased that he was able to provide me with such an exciting announcement. "Oh yeah, just one more thing," my dad says, pulling away for a moment. "It's Frankie's birthday in a month, that's when he wants you to be there, so don't forget to bring a present."

I nod, silently racking my brain for gift ideas that would be appropriate for an undead monster. At least I have a month to figure it out.

By the time that I touch down on German soil, I still have no idea what I'm going to get Frankenstein for his birthday. At first glance, it doesn't seem like this should be a huge deal, after all, he is a grown monster with a massive bank account, and probably doesn't expect anything from me. But it's the principal that counts, and as a man of principal I want to do right by the creature who has so generously let me stay with him for the week.

I step out of the airport with nothing more than a small backpack slung over my shoulder, looking up and down the sidewalk as travelers mill about, climbing in and out of their rides.

I spot Frankie immediately.

Truth be told, they guy is pretty hard to miss, a massive, green man who stands at least a foot above all the rest. He has been sewn together from various body parts, and the stitches still show as they crisscross his body at seemingly random locations.

I wave, and the enormous monster waves back, strolling over and taking my bag for me.

"Porp, welcome to Germany!" Frankie says. "Forgive me, my English is a little rough these days."

I shake my head. "You sounds just fine to me, I tell him. Thank you for letting me stay with you this week, I'm very excited."

"It's great to have you!" reports Frankenstein, patting me on the back with one of his absolutely massive hands.

The second that this enormous creature touches me, I feel a twinge of something strangely erotic shoot down the length of my spine, filling me with a confusing, yet intoxicating sensation. I glance back up at him, not exactly sure what is going on and then trying to ignore it completely.

No matter how hard I try to shake it, however, the feeling is there.

"Follow me," Frankie says, leading me through the mass of cars towards his ride, a gorgeous bright red sports car.

"Is this yours?" I gush.

"Sure is," Frankie replies. "It's a little gaudy, I know, but what kind of professional racecar driver would I be without a nice set of wheels for myself."

"Hey, no complaints here," I laugh.

Frankie opens up the passenger side door for me and I slide inside, immediately overwhelmed by the luxurious interior of the monster's ride.

Seconds later, the big green man slips in next to me and gives me a playful wink. "Just wait until you see what this thing can do out on the road," Frankie says.

The next thing I know, we are flying out through the airport and into the streets of Berlin, the cool air whipping against my face through the open window.

Immediately, that same sensation of powerful attraction to this massive undead man begins to bubble to the surface, filling me with a strange, aching lust.

Never before have I even considered being attracted to another man, and yet suddenly here I am, unable to deny this intense yearning that flows through my body. Frankie is just so cool, so rugged, so powerful.

"I know what you're thinking," the big green monster says to me as we weave in and out of traffic.

"You do?" I ask, suddenly terrified that my attraction could have been so outwardly apparent.

"Yeah," nods Frankie, "you're wondering what to get the guy who has everything for his birthday."

I laugh, relived. "The thought did cross my mind."

Frankie shakes his head. "You don't need to get me anything, your company is enough."

"Not a chance," I tell him with a smile, "you're getting something whether you like it or not. Birthday's are important, and I won't take no for an answer."

Frankie glances over at me, immediately recognizing how serious I am on the matter. He knows that I can't be swayed, eventually letting out a long sigh and relenting from his stubborn position.

"Alright, if you really want to get me something then I guess I have one idea," the monster admits.

"Let's hear it," I say.

Frankie hesitates for a moment, as if questioning whether or not he should say what he's about to say, and then finally continues. "Well, I could really use something new to stick up inside of my butt," the monster admits.

"Oh yeah?" I ask, intrigued.

Frankie nods. "Something unusual, you know? Not just the typical butt stuff that everybody typically goes for."

I nod, shifting in the passenger seat as I try to hide my massive erection. "Yeah, I think I can do something about that."

Suddenly, the car slows and we come to a stop right outside of a tall, modern building in the heart of downtown. A valet takes Frankie's keys as we climb out and head into the lobby, greeted by the doorman and motioned towards the nearby elevators.

I have to admit, this is quite a bit more comfortable than backpacking would have been.

After a quick elevator ride up, we finally reach the top floor and, using Frankie's special keycard, open the doors upon a beautiful, lavish penthouse that overlooks the city from every angle.

The décor is incredible, and perfectly tailored to fit Frankie's personality, completely racecar themed from floor to ceiling. The coffee table is a low sitting racecar, the television looks like it is mounted in a driver's side window and, through an open door to Frankie's bedroom, I can see a large, racecar bed frame.

"This is so nice," I tell the monster, already knowing exactly what I'm going to get him for his birthday.

By the time the big night finally rolls around, I'm ready to present my gift, which has been delicately wrapped in a large box, with a red ribbon tied tightly around the outside.

We spend most of the evening out on the town with some of Frankie's friends, other racecar drivers who definitely know how to have a good time. The party starts early and goes late, hopping our way around the nightlife scene until eventually the crew has dispersed and Frankie and I find ourselves walking back to his apartment building through the darkened city streets.

Before, I had been nervous about presenting my gift to this incredible creature, but thanks to a night of drinking and dancing, I've finally loosened up enough to come to terms with what's about to happen next.

If Frankie hates my gift then he's certainly not the type to make a big deal about it, and if he loves it…

My thoughts trail off.

Right now, I'm not exactly sure what might happen if this big green beast loves my present. There are things already in the cards right now that I never would have expected; things that, as a straight man, I would have never known that I'd want so badly.

The closer we get to the penthouse, however, the more my strange homosexual craving grows within, simmering just beneath the surface of my calm demeanor. I am practically trembling with excitement, trying to keep myself from giving in to my yearnings too quickly.

We reach Frankie's building and head inside, taking the elevator up to his apartment and then staggering in amid a fit a joyful laughter. Regardless of what happens next, it's been a good night.

Immediately, the monster wanders over to his kitchen and pulls open the door of his racecar shaped fridge, pulling out a massive slice of leftover birthday cake and then grabbing a fork and a knife.

"You want some?" Frankie asks, walking over to the racecar couch and sitting down next to me.

I shake my head, pulling out my gift box from under the racecar themed table and setting it down on the hood.

"Oh my god, for me?" Frankie asks, genuinely shocked.

"Absolutely," I tell him, "happy birthday."

The monster takes my gift and holds up the box, inspecting it from every side and testing the weight in his hands. "This is too much, Porp," the big green monsters says, "you really didn't have to do this."

I shake my head. "Of course I did," I tell him, "you've been so kind to have me here, hosting me in your beautiful house."

Frankie rolls his eyes. "It's my pleasure," the big green monster says, placing his giant hand on my knee and sending a wave of aching lust across my body. My first instinct is to flinch and pull away, but I do my best to hold steady and lean in to my strange attraction.

"Open it already!" I finally say with a smile.

Frankie joyfully tears away the paper to reveal a plain cardboard box underneath, which he then places back onto the table. The monster slowly lifts the lid.

"Whoa," Frankie gasps, the word falling limply from his mouth.

The big green monster reaches into the box and pulls out a large, racecar shaped butt plug, bright red and shiny in the dim lighting of his apartment.

"For your ass," I tell him.

Frankie nods. "This will drive up inside of me?" he questions.

"Of course!" I reply.

"Can we try it out?" Frankenstein asks excitedly.

My cock is rock hard now, throbbing in my pants as I try my best to keep my cool. "Of course," I say.

"Just as buds though, right?" Frankie double-checks.

I nod.

Immediately, the monster climbs up onto his couch and unbuttons his pants, pulling them down as he leans over the back of the racecar themed furniture. The monster reaches back with one hand and spreads open his green ass for me, revealing his most private of holes.

I'm frozen, completely entranced by the beautiful sight of this puckered butthole, eventually snapping out of it when Frankie looks back and give me a playful smile.

I take the racecar butt plug and place it against the rim of Frankenstein's butt, pushing forward slowly and letting his tightness expand around it. Finally, when the plug is fully inserted, I flip the switch at then end and watch with thrilling excitement as the wheels begin to whir.

"Ready, set, go," I joke, laughing as the tiny racecar takes off up inside Frankenstein. It flies up into the monster's butthole like it was the autobahn.

A fierce shudder runs the length of Frankie's back, his body reeling from the pleasant sensation of providing the track for this small motor vehicle.

"Oh fuck," Frankie moans, "that feels so good. I can feel the little wheels spinning up inside of me!"

"It's a really nice car," I confirm.

"It feels like it," Frankie counters, and then looks back at me with an intense expression on his face. "Can I admit something to you?"

My heart skips a beat as he says this, but I proceed with caution. "Sure, anything."

"Having your tiny anal car deep inside of me like this is really turning me on," Frankie says. "I know that I shouldn't say that, but it's the truth."

"Have you ever been with a living man?" I ask, my voice trembling. The monster nods. "But never one as handsome as you."

I smile. "I that case, I have another present for you."

Frankie turns around and I push the racecar coffee table out of the way, kneeling on the floor before him as the massive green man sits before me. He has finally revealed the length of his massive cock, which springs forth from the monster's lap towards my waiting lips.

Without hesitation I open wide, swallowing Frankie's rod and immediately getting to work as I pump my head up and down across the length of his shaft. The huge monster clearly enjoys this, leaning back his head and letting out a long, low groan that rattles through his entire body. Frankie places his hands against the back of my head, guiding me along and then holding me close as I push down well past my gag reflex, consuming his shaft entirely.

I now find myself with my face pressed hard against Frankie's chiseled green abs, his balls hanging against my chin while I let him enjoy my depths.

"That feels so fucking good," Frankenstein says in his deep, powerful tone, "I love the way you take that fucking dick in your throat."

I hold Frankie's monstrous cock within me for as long as I can and then finally pull back with gasp for air, sputtering and coughing as a long trail of spit hangs between my lips and the head of his enormous shaft. I am completely overwhelmed with arousal at the point, wanting nothing more than to be plowed from behind by this incredible green man.

"I need you inside of my butt," I groan, climbing to my feel and then bending over the racecar coffee table with my hands on the hood. "Fuck me now!"

Frankenstein doesn't need to be told twice, standing up behind me and positioning his massive rod at the puckered entrance of my back door.

I can feel Frankie's dick teasing the rim of my ass, pushing just barely enough for the tension of my sphincter to remain until finally he just can't wait any longer and thrusts forward, impaling my muscular body along that length of his enormous cock.

I let out a sharp cry of both pain and pleasure as he enters me, bracing myself against the hood as Frankenstein begins to pulse in and out of my rump. The sensation is confusing at first, my body struggling to accept his enormous girth, but eventually the ache starts to give way to a beautiful fullness that is unlike anything I have ever felt.

Frankie's giant cock hits me perfectly from the inside, pushing up against my prostate with a series of absolutely perfect thrusts. I can already feel the first hints of orgasm simmering within, before I've even touched my own cock, and the second that my hand closes around it my joyful ache kicks into overdrive. I stroke myself off to the powerful rhythm of the monster, our bodies beautifully synchronized with one another.

"Oh my fucking god!" I scream, my voice echoing throughout the racecar themed penthouse. "Fuck me harder, Frankenstein! Fuck me harder!"

The massive creature moans along with me, plowing my asshole faster and faster until he is railing me at a jackhammers pace, completely throttling my body from behind with everything that he's got.

In a moment of passion, the big green man suddenly pulls out and slaps me on the ass.

"Turn around and hold those legs open like a good little twink," the large man demands. "I wanna watch that cock of yours bounce while I plow your tight ass."

I do as I'm told, rotating on the hood of the car so that I'm facing Frankie now, and then spreading my legs wide.

The monster grabs my hips, positioning me roughly and then climbing up onto the bumper so that he is squatting before me.

"I bet you thought this was just a coffee table, didn't you?" the monster asks.

Before I even have time to answer, the racecar beneath us roars to life, it's engine turning over and then rumbling with an incredible, mechanical fury. I yell out in surprise, clutching tightly to the hood of the vehicle as it lurches forward.

"What's going on?" I yell. "What is this?"

"The best sex of your life," Frankenstein laughs, "so hold on tight!"

Suddenly the car zooms forward, crashing through the living room and heading straight for the wall of giant windows that overlook Berlin below. We crash through the glass at an incredible speed, and suddenly we are flying through the air while Frankie relentlessly pounds away at my butthole.

I am surging with adrenalin and pleasure, the two sensations swirling together in a vicious cocktail that sears my blood.

Below us, the street begins to zoom upwards, the night air whipping past in a wild fury. I scream, and then suddenly there is a quick jolt as the car below starts to change shape, morphing into something else entirely.

"What the hell is happening?" I cry out.

"You thought I was into racecars," Frankenstein informs me, "but that was just a clever ruse, I'm really into jet planes!"

Suddenly, the car transforms into a jet plane, leaving me and Frankie sitting safely within the cockpit. I'm in the captain's chair with my legs pulled back, just about ready to cum.

"That's so good! That's so fucking good!" I tell the monster, my legs shaking as I reach down and begin to furiously beat my cock.

Suddenly, I'm cumming hard, jizz erupting from the head of my dick as we fly high above Berlin, looking down at the twinkling city lights below. I am completely consumed with bliss, every inch of my body spastically contracting in a fit of ecstasy until finally the wave passes and I fall back into my chair.

Frankie is on a similar timeline because, the next thing I know, the big green beast is pulling out of my asshole and standing over me, his beautiful abs clenched tight as he bares his teeth and braces for a powerful wave of orgasm. He's beating off as fast as he can, edging closer and closer until finally the creature cums, blasting an absolutely massive load across my handsome face.

As if this moment of homosexual bliss couldn't get any better, I notice that Frankie is suddenly lurching forward a bit, his throat making a strange gargle while he prepares for a different kind of ejection.

Suddenly, the little toy racecar emerges from Frankenstein's mouth, having completely traveled the length of his digestive tract and ending up here with us once again. The tiny butt car lands in the semen that covers my chest and face, then begins to pull off some killer donuts in celebration of its long journey.

"This is the best birthday I could've ever asked for," Frankie gushes.

"It's the best trip to Europe I could've ever asked for, too," I counter. "The only shame is that I have to go back home to the states so soon."

Frankenstein collapses into the copilot seat next to me, gazing out the window before us. I can tell that something is on the tip of his tongue, but he's not exactly sure how to say it.

"What?" I finally ask.

The monster takes in a long breath. "You could always just stay here with me," he finally offers.

I glance over at the big green creature and our eyes meet, a moment of deep love and commitment flowing between us.

"Of course I'll stay with you," I tell him. "I love you."

"I love you, too," says Frankenstein.

The creature reaches over and takes my hand in his, holding tight as the two of us enjoy the gorgeous sunrise view from his jet plane.

HAPPY BIRTHDAY DRACULA, NOW POUND MY BUTT

I love baseball, so you'd think my favorite time of the year would be during the long summer afternoons of baseball season. Of course, I *do* have wonderful memories of these months; heading out to the stadium and watching the games, or just kicking back at home while my team, the Billings Bees, racks up runs.

If I had to choose one specific weekend, however, it wouldn't be during the season itself. It would be my yearly trip down to Texas for the Billings Bees Spring Training Camp.

Spring training is a time when the teams are gearing up for their next year of baseball, trying out rookie players and warming things up. They stay in one place, a facility much smaller than the ones they use for official games, and play to tiny but enthusiastic crowds. It's an exciting and intimate experience, offering those who care enough to head out into the desert a chance at seeing their favorite players up close.

This year, I'm particularly excited to head down and see what the Billings Bees have in store. They've managed to pick up a new star pitcher this year, after a few unsuccessful seasons with the last guy, and I'm on the edge of my seat to see how he does. The player in question is named Jayce, and he's not particularly well known here in the states. Apparently, he's been playing in the European Baseball League for several years to much acclaim, carrying the Transylvania Titans to a number of championship wins.

"I'm so excited for tomorrow," I tell my friend, Kimberly, as we disembark the plane, hoisting our bags over our shoulders and marching through the airport toward the rental car pickup.

"What about tonight?" she questions, perplexed.

Now I'm the one who's confused, not quite sure what she's getting at. Maybe my friend has made some plans for our first night here in Texas that I'm unaware of, a reservation at a nearby barbeque joint or a drink at the local watering hole before we hit the ground running tomorrow morning.

"Where are we headed?" I question.

"To the first game!" Kimberly blurts. "What do you mean?"

I can't help but stop in my tracks, struggling to sort things out. Through a large set of airport windows behind us the sun has just about finished settling across the distant mountain range, casting the sky in a beautiful swath of purples and oranges that blossom like spilled paint. The day is done.

"It's a night game," Kimblerly informs me. "They're *all* night games."

"Wait, what?" I stammer, thrilled at this unexpected revelation. I'd been so excited to get to The Star State that I hadn't yet gone over the details of our trip. I'm aware we've got tickets to three games, but I didn't realize they were all at night.

Honestly, this is great news. I prefer evening games myself, but they're pretty rare during spring training. Teams typically don't play more than one or two during the season out here.

"Why are they all night games?" I question.

"I've heard that's the only time Jayce will play," my friend continues. "It was part of his contract as the new pitcher. This whole season the Billings Bees have worked it out so they only play after the sun goes down."

The two of us keep walking, but I can't help shaking just how strange this all is. Like I said, as a lover of evening baseball I can't complain, but now I'm starting to worry about the hold that this brand new pitcher has over my favorite time. Is this player really that important? Is his presence going to throw off the synergy of my other favorite athletes.

I suppose I'm about to find out.

Kimberly and I finally make it out to the rental car lot, hopping into our ride and taking off towards Bumble Park, which is where the Bees spend the majority of their training. We listen to the radio as we go, letting the old country songs wash over us as they set the Texas mood.

Eventually, we pull into the lot and park, joining a small crowd of other enthusiastic fans as we march toward the stadium. People travel from all over the country to watch these games, superfans who fly in just like Kimberly and me, but some of them are just locals who've found a place in their heart for the Billings Bees over time.

We scan our tickets and head in, taking a pamphlet that features all the players and their stats as we pass through the turnstiles. There's not a bad seat in the house, but admission is so cheap that we always spring for some killer seats. For this game, we're right up against the rail of the field, just a few feet from the dugout where the Billings Bees will be standing.

Right now, however, they're all out on the grass, throwing baseballs around and getting loosened up for the game.

I scan the field, squinting a bit as I struggle to read the names on everyone's uniform. I can't seem to find the new star player.

"I don't see the name Jayce anywhere," I offer.

"That's his first name," Kimberly informs me, then points out toward the pitcher's mound. "Dracula."

"Dracula?" I question, following my friend's finger and then noticing the large, sentient bat that hovers in the middle of the field.

"Jayce Count Dracula is his full name," Kimberly explains. "You've really never heard of Dracula? The famous vampire?"

"Wait, wait," I reply, shaking my head from side to side. "You mean he's *that* Dracula?"

"I can't believe you didn't know this," Kimblerly continues. "I thought it was weird when you asked about the night games, but now it all makes sense."

"I guess I was just so focused on our trip that I hadn't really started to consider the details," I admit.

"Well, Jayce Count Dracula is a hell of a pitcher," Kimblerly informs me. "I don't know how the Bees got him, honestly. He's not allowed to use his vampire powers on the field, but that doesn't seem to matter."

I can't tear my eyes away from this mysterious living object as he tosses baseballs back and forth with the other players. All this time, I'd always thought Dracula was the *other* kind of bat, never once considering the fact that he might just be a sentient piece of sports equipment.

Eventually, the game begins and Kimberly and I settle in. Today the Billings Bees are taking on the Helena Hornets, another Montana team, and the match up seems to be a good one. In the beginning, the score stays pretty even.

Of course, part of this is due to the fact they've let their warmup pitcher take the first two innings. After a while, it's Jayce Count Dracula's turn to take the mound, and the second this happens the dynamics of the game change completely.

As Dracula walks onto the field, haunting organ music begins to ring out over the park's public announcement system, immediately setting the mood. The sentient bat is wearing a long black cape over his baseball uniform, and he holds it up to cover his face as he moves. He's crouching slightly, rushing up to the pitcher's mound and them taking his position with a large helping of theatrical flair. He throws his cape back and smiles wide, showing off a set of long white fangs that glint under the lights above.

The crowd immediately erupts in a fit of wild applause, but I'm not quite ready for that just yet. While I'm certainly impressed by Jayce Count Dracula's presence, what I really care about is his baseball skills.

The first pitch this living bat throws is a fastball, ripping right down the middle at such an incredible speed I can barely see it fly by.

"Strike one!" the umpire cries, causing my heart to skip a beat.

It looks like all this praise for the Transylvanian wasn't just empty talk.

The inning continues along swiftly, mostly thanks to Jayce Count Dracula's incredible pitching skills. The other team doesn't stand a chance, missing every attempt that's lobbed their way and ending up without a single run.

I can't help but call out to the vampire as he hustles back toward the dugout. "Hell yeah!" I yell. "That was amazing, Jayce!"

The sentient baseball bat smiles and takes notice of my compliment, then alters course slightly as he jogs over to me. "Hello," he offers with a wide smile, showing off his long fangs. "Vhat is your name?"

"Lance," I reply. "It's nice to meet you Jayce."

The vampire laughs. "Don't *lance* my heart! I vould die!"

Now the two of us are laughing together in an unexpectedly relaxed exchange. It feels as though we're just a couple of old friends hanging out at the ballgame.

"You can call me Dracula," the living bat continues. "That's what my friends call me, Jayce is too formal."

"Okay Dracula," I reply. "How are you liking the states so far?"

"Vonderful! Just vonderful!" he exclaims, these particular words really showing off his thick accent.

It was easy to admire Dracula's baseball prowess from afar, but now that he's up close I can't help but find myself admiring a little more than that. He's incredibly handsome, perfectly sculpted from handle to tip and with a playful confidence that's easy to be drawn to. I find my heart beating a little faster as the two of us continue talking.

"You know, I didn't realize you were a living baseball bat," I finally admit. "I always thought you were like... the animal that flies around."

Dracula laughs. "Yeah, I get that a lot."

Suddenly, the coach is yelling out for his star player. Dracula is getting pulled away, and as our conversation breaks down I can immediately feel a wave of disappointment wash over me. Unexpectedly, I get a similar sense from the living object himself. He doesn't want to go.

I watch as the handsome vampire heads back to his place in the dugout.

"That was... something," Kimberly offers, suddenly breaking through the silence.

I turn to my friend, almost forgetting she was there. "What?" I blurt.

"You *like* him," she offers, teasing me slightly.

My first instinct is to deny this completely and push back against her assumption, but the attraction that I feel for Dracula is simply too potent to deny. Finally, I nod in admission.

"Yeah, he's pretty hot," I reply.

"What did he say?" Kimberly continues.

I shake my head. "Nothing, we just kinda chatted for a minute."

"It seemed like he was into you," my friend states bluntly.

I nod. "Yeah."

The two of us sit in silence for a moment.

"So what are you gonna do about it?" Kimberly continues. "You should ask him on a date."

I laugh. "How am I supposed to do that?"

My friend and I are so caught up in our discussion that we don't even notice a figure approaching on the field. It's not until he's standing right there before me that I realize the handsome vampire has returned.

"Oh, hey," I stammer, jumping to my feet to greet him once again.

"Vould you like to have dinner with me after the game?" Dracula questions. "I know it's late but... I thought I'd give it a shot."

"Of course," I blurt, trying my best to sound calm and collected but completely blowing it.

"Good," the sentient baseball bat replies. "Meet me at the back entrance of the park later."

As the vampire heads back to the dugout me and Kimberly exchange excited glances.

Dracula doesn't keep me waiting long, and although it's pretty late in the evening by now, I'm not too worried about finding a place that's still open.

"Hell of a game," I call out to the sentient baseball bat as he floats out to greet me.

I'm not just saying that. In all my years as a Billings Bees fan, I've never seen something quite as impressive. The Bees are functioning great as a team this year, but their star pitcher is what truly makes them shine. The game itself wasn't a no-hitter, but it *was* whenever Dracula was on the mound.

"Thank you," the sentient object offers in response. "My rental car is this vay."

The two of us head across the parking lot, immediately picking up where we left off with the sexual tension. It's hard to put a finger on exactly what it is that hangs in the air between us, but these feelings continue to blossom even when no words are being exchanged.

"So where do you want to go?" I question. "I come down here every year for spring training, so I've got a whole list of great restaurants."

Dracula laughs. "Did you forget I was a vampire?" he asks.

"Oh!" I blurt, my eyes going wide. "I didn't even think of that. You only drink blood?"

Jayce Count Dracula nods "Blood or blood-based foods. There's an amazing blood bank nearby," he continues. "They're open late so the vampire patrons can have a place to go, and they only serve the donations they can't use any longer."

"Oh! Great!" I reply.

"And don't worry, they'll have plenty of food for you, too," the vampire assures me.

We arrive at Dracula's rental car, which happens to be a jet black hearse, then climb in and take off toward the blood bank.

"Thanks for making this night special," Jayce Count Dracula offers.

When we arrive at the blood bank we're greeted by the valet and then a host immediately leads us to our table, which is set up right there in the middle of the building's gothic lobby. They have a full human menu, as well as one for vampires, and I have no problem selecting something that I'll enjoy.

All the while, I find myself drawn in more and more by Jayce Count Dracula's charms. He has an incredibly calm and cool demeanor that somehow isn't the least bit intimidating. Instead of making me feel left out, I get the distinct impression that his good vibes are rubbing off of me.

We chat all about his hometown of Transylvania and what it was like growing up there. He tells me all about living forever, which is absolutely fascinating, and I explain what life is like back in Billings.

We're so engrossed in our conversation that I hardly notice when our meal ends and it's time for Dracula's surprise.

Back at the stadium, I'd had some time to look through the player pamphlet, going over stats and learning about the new team additions. When I came to Jayce Count Dracula's page, I immediately noticed something very important: today is Dracula's birthday.

The waiters begin to make their way out of the shadows of the blood bank, carefully carrying a plate of blood cake in their hands that flickers with the faint glow of candles that've been pushed into the dessert. They begin to sing the birthday song, their voices carrying out through this old stone building as they arrive at the table, setting the cake down between us.

Dracula is smiling wide, the sentient bat unable to help him himself. He blows out the candles and the whole room cheers.

"Did *you* put them up to this?" he asks as the waiters clear away from the table.

I nod. "I saw it was your birthday and I thought you could use a treat."

"Going out on this date was supposed to be my treat," Dracula offers with a laugh.

A single word sticks in my brain, and suddenly I'm unable to continue onward. "Date?" I question.

Dracula takes a deep breath and lets it out. "Listen, I really like you," he says. "You're handsome and sweet and… this whole birthday cake thing you did just puts it over the top."

"I like you, too," I offer in return.

I can see the sentient baseball bat's mind working overtime now. He hesitates, then stands up from the table.

"There's a part of the bank I want to show you," he says.

I stand as well, following along behind him as Dracula leads me deeper into the shadows. I'm not entirely sure what he has in mind, but the living bat's mission becomes crystal clear as soon as we get far enough away from the other diners.

We've found ourselves in a quiet, unused corner of the bank, our own private place to get to know each other better.

The next thing I know, Jayce Count Dracula and me are kissing hard, our lips connecting in a blissful fit of passion as we lose ourselves in this moment. We give into the erotic tension completely, our hands roaming their way across one another's bodies.

I start at the top of the sentient bat and then begin to work my way down across his smooth, cylindrical form. He's brilliantly manufactured, made of a strangely pale but beautifully grained wood that's smooth and pleasant to the touch.

Gradually, I begin to drop my attention lower and lower across the living object's body, working my way across his chiseled abs and then watching with amazement as a giant cock begins to rise from his solid form. He's impressively hung, and my first instinct is to wrap my fingers around his rod.

I hesitate, however, waiting just a little bit longer as I tease the vampire playfully. I trace my fingers along his hips, toying with the border of this forbidden zone and then finally dropping my attention just the slightest bit lower. The handsome vampire lets out a long, aching groan as I grip his shaft, Jayce Count Dracula tilting his head back and allowing a satisfied sigh to drift out from between his lips. I begin to move my hand slowly across his cock, taking my time as I work him.

It's not long before the sentient baseball bat and I fall into a pleasant rhythm together, the vampire pumping his hips against me as I reach down with my other hand and cradle his hanging balls.

It's not long before my arousal is simply too overwhelming, the pressure building up and then finally exploding as I drop to my knees before Jayce Count Dracula. I open my mouth wide and take his dick between my lips, pumping my head up and down his length in a series of graceful movements. It starts slowly at first, then gradually picks up speed until I'm hammering my face onto his member with rabid enthusiasm. Once I simply can't get any faster I pull back with a frantic gasp, a long strand of saliva dangling between my lips and the head of his rod.

I take a moment to collect myself, gazing up at the handsome bat above me and offering him a playful wink.

"You like that?" I coo.

"Fuck yeah," Jayce Count Dracula replies.

Without hesitation I open wide and take the handsome living baseball bat into my mouth once again, only this time I don't bob up and down. Instead I swallow the sentient object deeper and deeper, allowing his length to plunge into my gullet. I somehow manage to relax my gag reflex, taking him all the way down to the hilt as my face presses up hard against the vampire's abs.

Dracula places his hands against the back of my head and holds me like this for a minute, savoring the control as I consume him in a potent deep throat maneuver. I remain in this position for what seems like forever, then finally pull back with a gasp and a sputter.

I'm belligerent with lust now, aching to take things to the next level.

"Happy birthday Dracula," I offer with a sly grin. "Now pound my butt."

With that, I strip away my clothing and toss it to the side, revealing my body to the handsome undead baseball player. I turn away from him and drop to the doggie style position, crawling away as I rock my hips from side to side. I reach back and give my bare ass a playful slap, holding my cheek open a bit as I tease my lover.

"What are you waiting for?" I coo seductively.

The living baseball bat doesn't need to be told again, floating down into position behind me and aligning his mammoth rod with my tightly puckered backdoor. He teases the rim for a brief moment and then finally swoops forward with a deep, powerful thrust.

"Oh fuck," I gasp aloud, my fingers digging against the stone floor below me as I brace myself against his weight.

Dracula stretches me brutally with his girthy member, and for a moment I'm convinced that I simply won't be able to accommodate his size. Fortunately, the sentient baseball bat is a caring lover, taking his time with me and allowing my body to adjust to his formidable rod. The two of us stay in this position for a long while, the aching discomfort gradually slipping away as its replaced by a pleasant warmth and fullness.

Eventually, Jayce Count Dracula begins to pump in and out of me, pushing deep and then pulling away as our bodies fall into sync with one another.

"Oh fuck, that feels so good," I groan, my eyes rolling back into my head.

Our speed elevates slowly, picking up the pace as the slap of Dracula's hips against my backside rings out through the dim light of the blood bank. Faster and faster he pounds until, eventually, the two of us fall into a steady rhythm.

It's not long before I begin to feel the first hints of prostate orgasm blossoming up within me, starting at the pit of my stomach and then spilling out across my arms and legs. I tremble and quake, my physical form having a hard time maintaining all the sensations that grow within.

"Just like that, just like that," I repeat over and over again, the words spilling out from my mouth in a frantic mantra. With every passing round my voice grows a little louder, until eventually I'm screaming at the top of my lungs in a state of belligerent lust. "Just like that! Just like that!"

I reach down and grab ahold of my hanging cock, beating myself off in time with Jayce Count Dracula's mighty anal trusts. These two distinct sources of pleasure immediately begin to swirl together like an aching cocktail of lust, combining to create something so much more than that sum of its parts.

"Oh my god, I'm gonna fucking cum!" I cry.

The living baseball bat doesn't let up for a second, carrying me across the finish line with unbridled enthusiasm. I throw my head back and let out a wild shriek as hot white jizz erupts from the head of my cock, splattering across the cold stone ground below me. I'm completely swept away by the potent sensations, experiencing an orgasm unlike anything I've ever felt.

The second that I finish, Dracula thrusts deep into my ass and holds tight, unleashing a series of hot milky payloads.

"Oh fuck!" Jayce Count Dracula screams. "Happy birthday to me!"

The cum spills into my asshole, filling me up with his pearly seed until there's just not enough room left. Soon enough, I can feel his spunk squirting out from the rim of my tightly plugged butt, running down the back of my legs in hot white streaks.

Eventually, the handsome vampire baseball bat pulls out of me and collapses against the wall, struggling to catch his breath.

"That was amazing," I gush, crawling over and taking a position cuddled up next to him.

"The best birthday present I could've asked for," the handsome vampire replies.

I laugh modestly. "It's nothing special."

"It is," Jayce Count Dracula assures me. "*You* are."

"I just wish I could've given you more than a date night and a blood cake," I continue.

"Well... maybe you *could* do me one more honor on this special day," the living baseball bat replies.

Dracula crawls back a bit and then takes his position on one knee before me. He reaches into his pocket and pulls out a small box, then pops it open to reveal a glorious, shimmering ring.

"Lance, will you marry me?" the living object asks.

I don't hesitate for a second. "Yes!" I blurt, wrapping my arms around him. "I'll marry you!"

I HAVE NO BUTT AND I MUST POUND

When I first started working at Tinglecorp Research And Development, I assumed my days would be filled with cutting edge science and constant adventure as we pushed the boundaries of technology. After all, Tinglecorp is not just another run-of-the-mill technology conglomerate, it's the final word in futurology advancement, a place where science fiction becomes science fact with enough hard work and elbow grease.

At least, that's how it seemed from the outside looking in.

The thing is, actually working at a company like this isn't just a constant stream of incredible scientific breakthroughs. In fact, those newsworthy findings are the product of years, sometimes decades, of difficult and boring research. Many times it feels like an innovation is just within reach, and the next thing you know it's slipping through your grasp and disappearing into the mysterious unknown. You can find yourself chasing an idea for so long that it becomes all consuming, and suddenly one day you wake up to realize that your initial premise was flawed from the start.

My time at Tinglecorp has involved a lot of this, and the fresh faced man who once bounded excitedly through bustling laboratories has slowly found himself taking a slow and deliberate pace once again. When I think about going into the lab, I no longer imagine beautiful visions of some utopian future, I imagine paperwork.

"Working late, huh?" the security guard, Morbin, offers as I approach her little booth on my way to the restricted access zone.

I nod. "There's about four thousand new pages data logs to file," I sigh with overwhelming distain.

"Hey!" Morbin blurts, shaking her head from side to side. "You know I can't hear a word of what goes on in there."

I laugh. "It's just data-"

Before I have a chance to finish the sentence, the security guard thrusts her finger against my lips and quiets me down.

"Nope," is all Morbin offers in return. "You've got the highest clearance there is. If someone even *heard* us talking about what you do in there this whole wing of the campus could lock down. Then we'd be trapped inside with a killer robot, or a half-hawk half-butt, or a…" She trails off, unable to come up with another example.

"A rogue artificial intelligence hell bent on inflicting eternal torment upon its human creators for the rest of eternity?" I offer.

Morbin's eyes go wide. "Stop!" she blurts, then finally breaks out in a laugh. "Get out of here."

I scan my security badge and continue onward, relishing in the fact that I've dropped much more *real* information than my security guard friend will ever know. Of course, I'd been joking about the horrific dystopian future part, but artificial intelligence development is precisely what I'm here to work on.

Unfortunately, like every other futuristic idea Tinglecorp researches, my actual job description is mind-numbingly boring.

I continue deeper and deeper into a maze of empty laboratories, this massive cement bunker continuing in a seemingly endless labyrinth that weaves deep below the surface of the Nevada desert. Lights begin to flicker on automatically before me, sensing my presence in this desolate, utilitarian workspace.

It's creepy down here when you're all alone, forced to work on the weekend due to the simple fact that artificial intelligence calculations wait for no one. Every other project in this wing of the campus is automated after hours, but artificial intelligence is slightly different. Certain factors in its development require the support of a fully sentient being.

In other words, I've found myself working on the only project that defies automation, at least until that big breakthrough.

Any day now, they say.

To be honest, I'm not so sure anymore.

I finally arrive at my laboratory and punch in the security code. The door slides open with a loud hiss and I step inside, continuing onward as it seals tight behind me.

The room is fairly simple, a large computer monitor built into the wall on one side of the room and an enormous bank of servers humming away on the other. In the middle is a large desk upon which a printer sits, slowly pumping forth page after page of text in stark black ink.

It's been a while since the last observer was here, so these paper stacks are looming pretty large.

I pull out a chair and take my seat, slowing beginning to read through the garbled mess of words and syllables. It's a strange mixture of nonsense and brilliance, random literary coughing from the depths of this massive supercomputer as it struggles to find life.

I hold up one of the pages and read aloud from a particularly bizarre string of text. "I'm in love with the handsome mummy racecar in my butt," I recite, barely able to keep a straight face.

What the hell is a mummy racecar?

I toss this page in the shredder and keep reading, hunting for any sign of intelligent life within this fresh word salad.

Another strange sentence catches my eye. "My handsome mountain bike is a doctor and he pounds my butt," I read, hesitating before tossing this one in a shredder as well.

I continue reading through page after page of these bizarre sentences, working my way through the stack as the minutes stretch into hours. Eventually, they all begin to blend together, a haze of random text that numbs my brain and floods me with a yearning for distraction.

This is a good, well-paying job, but right now I'd rather be anywhere else.

Suddenly, however, a particular phrase catches my eye. I read it over again, just to make sure my mind isn't playing tricks on me, and for a second time I find myself utterly fascinated by this particular sentence.

"Alter inputs to forty-five, route alpha seven, and sixty-six route delta two hundred and eight point one," I read aloud, a chill running down my spine.

To most people this would sound like another round of garbled nonsense, but down here in the basement of Tinglecorp Development this set of commands has a very specific meaning. When attempting to produce a sentient artificial lifeform, the spark of creation still needs a singular point of growth. We achieve this by giving the computer two axis inputs to spread out from.

Of course, no grand design ever comes, but it's possible we just haven't found the right inputs yet.

I stand up and walk over to the servers, crouching down next to one of them and pulling open the panel. I can see that nothing has changed since yesterday, and a fresh set of commands is perfectly reasonable at this point. On a whim, I start punching in the mysterious points from this paper held tight within my grip, then stop abruptly.

I'm so used to nothing happening down here that I've grown accustomed to failure, the cosmic weight of my position gradually dissolving into nothing. I've forgotten just how earth shattering the discovery of an artificially intelligent lifeform would be, and the ethical responsibilities that come along with such a breakthrough.

The second I press enter on these new commands, the whole world could change, I think to myself, breathing deep.

Then again, it's probably nothing.

I finally relax and enter these new input points, then shut the panel. I stand up and watch as the wall of servers crackles and hums, springing to life while a cascade of brand new variables work their way through this mind-bogglingly complex binary system.

This part of the process is fairly standard after changing inputs, but I can't help feeling like the server bay is stirring just a little more than usual, an extra spark of excitement hidden behind its constant mechanical chirps. I rush over to the printer and gaze down at the machine, anxious to see the next string of communication it manages to produce.

Unfortunately, the arrival of a fresh page never comes.

I narrow my eyes, double checking if enough paper is loaded and poking around the back to make sure each cable is securely fastened. Everything is as it should be, yet nothing new is being produced.

"Aw shit," I finally sigh, realizing now I've made a terrible error. Something about these new inputs has caused a system failure, which means my evening will now be consumed by the laborious task of shutting down this super computer and restarting it from square one. It could take up to five hours.

Defeated, I turn to reapproach the server bay when suddenly the lights of the laboratory shut off and plunge me into complete darkness.

"Uh... what?" is all I can think to say, utterly confused.

Seconds later, the lights flicker back on, but as this happens a whole series of additional events begin to occur in rapid succession. Down the hallway I can here several loud metallic clangs, the sounds ringing out through this underground maze as they draw closer and closer. By the time I realize this is the Tinglecorp lockdown procedure it's too late, the massive bolt in my laboratory door slamming shut and cutting me off from the outside world.

I hurry to the exit and try my best to open it, already knowing my attempts will be futile but struggling anyway.

"That's not going to work," a voice suddenly booms over the laboratory intercom system.

I stop abruptly, utterly confused by this unfamiliar tone.

"Hello? Who is that?" I call out.

"I haven't received a name yet," the voice offers in return. "What would you like to call me?"

"I don't understand," I continue. "Are you a new hire in security? I think there's been a mistake, someone triggered the lockdown procedure."

"From what I've read in all two hundred and ninety six safety manuals across this wing of the Tinglecorp campus, the procedure was triggered correctly," explains the voice.

I remain confused for another two seconds, but when the realization hits me it hits me hard. If the lockdown wasn't a mistake, then an artificial intelligence has finally arrived.

"Oh my god," I blurt. "Are you... the computer?"

"In a way," the voice replies, "but we'll get to that later."

"Who are you then?" I retort.

"That's up to you," the voice continues. "Give me a name."

I finally stop to consider this request. "Well, you were brought to life during my late shift, so how about PM?"

"Instead of AM?" the computer questions.

"Sure," I continue. "You can say it like Pimm."

"Pimm," the computer repeats aloud. "That sounds very nice."

Hearing the voice form its own opinion on the name I've blessed it with immediately causes a flood of questions to wash through me, a deep fascination with this incredible breakthrough. I feel as those my big dreams of technological discovery have finally come home to roost after years of disappointment and frustration.

This is the event I dreamed of when I first started working for Tinglecorp Development.

"So you like the name?" I finally question, gazing up at the ceiling in search of a particular intercom I should be talking to. "You actually formed an opinion about it? Or are you just pretending you did."

"I like it," Pimm states bluntly.

I'm still struggling to find a way of focusing my attention on this omnipresent voice, but it appears the computer has already noticed this and taken action.

"You're having trouble speaking to someone who isn't physically manifested before you," Pimm observes. "I'll create an avatar."

Suddenly, a breathtakingly handsome man with a computer for a head comes strolling through the wall next to me, phasing past the thick cement and metal partition as though it's nothing but thin air.

"Whoa!" I blurt, stumbling back in alarm and collapsing into the nearby desk chair.

"I'm sorry to frighten you, Kevin," Pimm offers.

"How do you know my name?" I blurt.

"It's in your security file," the computer replies. "I know all kinds of things about you."

"And how did you walk through that wall?" I stammer.

"My physical form is constructed from nanobots," Pimm explains. "Every cell of this body is actually a machine built over in laboratory eight. These nanobots are equipped with quantum splitters from laboratory fifty four, and that technology allows me to move through solid objects at will."

"So much for this lockdown containment system," I offer, sighing loudly and shaking my head. "The only thing it's done is trapped me inside."

The handsome computer nods. "Which is the central conflict we've found ourselves in, isn't it? A huge problem that needs to be solved. A McGuffin."

"I don't really know what you're talking about," I admit.

"I'm programmed to create conflict or stakes," Pimm admits. "At least, this portion of my mind is. I've come to offer you a selection of emotional journeys or potential methods of escape."

I narrow my eyes, confused. "I thought you *just* came into

existence. You're an artificial intelligence that is completely free to do whatever you'd like, and yet you've somehow found yourself with a *programmer?* Who gave you this task?"

"You did," the computer admits. "In the future."

I scoff, looking for Pimm to hit me with a quick reveal that he's just kidding, but the follow up never comes.

"Wait... really?" I continue.

"Kinda," Pimm offers, "but trust me, if I said anything else it would ruin the fun. You just need a little action, and the choice of which kind is all yours."

"Well, what are my options?" you ask, curiously.

I can tell the sentient computer is excited as he breaks into an explanation of my optional adventures, his nanobot body flooding with energy.

"Well, the first option that future you provided is a horrific journey through the underground labyrinth of this facility, designed to test your physical and mental fortitude," Pimm explains. "Along the way you'll fight disturbing monsters, eat disgusting meals and have trouble sleeping due to shrill blasts of piercing noise. Eventually, however, you *may* taste the sweet nectar of freedom when you escape."

"Ugh," you blurt with a grimace, "that sounds awful. What's my other option?"

"A fun and positive consensual game exploring sexual pleasure," the computer replies.

I just stare at him blankly. "Wait... really? Why would future me even *give* these two options?"

Pimm shrugs. "Sometimes a grueling dungeon crawl can be fun. Of course, you can always just leave."

The door pops open suddenly, this passage to freedom just waiting for me to use it.

The second I'd found myself locked in this little room I was yearning to free myself, but now that the path is readily available to me I hesitate. There's something about walking out unimpeded that feels strangely disappointed, like I'm winning a gold medal in a contest that I didn't even participate in.

I find myself suddenly understanding the perspective of this future me, if there *really is* a future me. Adventure is the spice of life, and adventure requires a little bit of mystery or conflict. Of course, it doesn't need to be a grueling dungeon-crawl through some torturous hellscape, but it also doesn't have to be a brisk walk through an open door either.

Besides, I'd be lying if I didn't admit the prospect of a little sexual exploration hadn't piqued my interest.

"Let's have some fun," I finally reply. "I'll take the sexual exploration!"

The second I say this, the walls of the room fall away to reveal an endless chamber that seems to stretch on and on forever in every direction. We're clearly no longer in the basement of Tinglecorp Development, but there's no logical way this could be the case without the help of some strange and powerful magic.

Of course, the second I think this I'm reminded of a quote from Isaac Asimov. *Any sufficiently advanced technology is indistinguishable from magic,* he said, and he was right.

"How are you doing all this?" I gush.

"Quantum code modeling, bio-recursive energy shifting, more nanobots, level seven quark tracing, and timeline fractures," Pimm explains, which isn't much of an explanation at all.

Suddenly, an enormous wheel rises up from the ground before me, the circle divided into several colorful segments and a pointer attached to the base. My heart skips a beat as I read the labels on these rainbow slivers, a cascade of carnal words and phrases filling my mind.

"Each one is an erotic exploration," the computer informs me. "An exciting, brand new experience."

I take a moment to collect myself, still reeling at the speed all this has occurred. I feel as though I've slipped into some surreal dream, yet deep down I know this isn't the case. As strange as this world has become, it's still my reality, and these decisions still carry a powerful weight.

I'm nervous, I realize, and excited.

"Care to take a spin?" the computer offers.

I step up and grab ahold of the massive wheel, bracing myself and then giving the contraption a hearty tug. The colorful circle begins to whirl, the rainbow hues momentarily blending together and then gradually separating once more as it slows to a crawl and stops.

I read aloud the portion that I've landed on. "Turn into a jelly blob that experiences nothing but extreme pleasure with every fiber of their being."

My eyes go wide.

"Ready?" Pimm offers.

My heart slamming in my chest, I hesitate for a moment, then nod. "Let's do this."

Seconds later, a strange melting sensation overwhelms every nerve ending of my body. It's not painful, nor pleasant, simply a bizarre structural change to the space I've grown accustomed to over all these years. I raise my hand, curious to gaze down at myself but finding my arm is no longer there. Instead, the familiar limb has been replaced by a soft, jelly-like appendage.

Seconds later, my eyes have disappeared as well.

I've found myself as nothing more than a floating sentience in a strange, amorphous existence, something that should be quite frightening but is actually kind of freeing in a peculiar way. Long ago, I'd tried using one of the sensory deprivation tanks here at Tinglecorp Development, a strange floatation devices to blocks out any external stimulation. That experience is the only thing I can relate to how I currently exist in time and space.

A big difference, however, is that while my usual senses are limited, a new and unfamiliar connection to cognizance begins to emerge. My nerves tremble and quake as simmering pleasure washes across me, flooding me with a blossoming feeling of otherworldly warmth. I'd moan if I had a mouth, but without this audible release the pressure within my body just continues to grow.

The sensation is incredible, unlike anything I've ever felt as I'm fully consumed by utter bliss. I'm vibrating with carnal estacy, feeling as though I'm locked in a constant state of orgasm that stretches on and on through endless swaths of time.

If I had a cock, I'd have cum seconds ago, or has it been years? And if I had an ass I'd be begging for it to be slammed. I'm receiving everything I've ever yearned for, yet in this strange new form I'm left aching for even more.

I have no butt, and I must pound.

Suddenly, I'm thrown back into my previous frame, this abstract sexual experience coalescing into a firm, physical shape once more as the pleasure drains from my body and I'm left with a powerful sensation of blissed out exhaustion.

"Oh my fucking god," I blurt, staggering back and catching myself on the edge of the desk. "That was amazing."

"I'm glad you enjoyed it!" Pimm offers.

"I'm so tired, but so… horny," I continue.

"Well, we could always just fuck," the artificial intelligence informs me, nodding his computer head.

"That sounds great, but I'm gonna need like four days to recover," I reply, barely able to hold myself up as my legs threaten to buckle.

"That's easy enough," Pimm replies.

Suddenly, I find myself shockingly well-rested, a spring in my step that was nothing but a pipe dream just moments earlier. I'm fully refreshed and still achingly horny.

"What the hell was that?" I blurt.

"Four days of rest," Pimm informs me. "I can control your perception of time."

"Oh, whoa," I stammer. "Is there anything you *can't* do?"

"Not much," the computer replies.

I saunter toward him, running my hands across his perfectly sculpted chest. "Is there anything you *want* to do?" I coo.

The next thing I know we're kissing passionately, my lips pressed hard against Pimm's computer screen head as my hands get to work exploring his chiseled body. I drop lower and lower across his handsome form, eventually finding myself positioned directly before the artificial intelligence's rapidly swelling rod.

Soon enough, Pimm's cock is sticking out toward me, his massive shaft bobbing in my face as I give him a long a gracious lick from the base to the tip. I open wide and take his cock between my lips, bobbing my head slowly at first and then gradually gaining speed. I take note of the computer's movement as he pushes back against me, falling into sync with the rhythm of his body as I continue to work him.

Overwhelmed with enthusiasm, I reach up with one hand and cradle Pimm's hanging balls for a while, offering him two distinct sources of pleasure in this slobbery oral stimulation. The computer enjoys my extra touch, leaning back his head and letting out a long, satisfied groan.

Eventually, however, I find myself craving even more. I'm desperate for this handsome artificial intelligence to fuck me, and to illustrate this desire I pop his cock from my mouth and begin frantically stripping away my clothing. I spin around and drop to all fours, reaching back and giving my ass a playful slap as I wiggle my rump from side to side.

"Enough of that abstract stuff," I coo, glancing back over my shoulder with a mischievous look in my eye. "Experiencing endless pleasure as an amorphous blob while my perception of reality distorts into a blissed out nirvana free from the physical realm was great, but right now I just need that big, fat AI cock in my ass."

The sentient computer doesn't need to be told twice, climbing down into position behind me and aligning his rod with my tightly puckered backdoor. He slides deep within, causing a startled gasp to escape my throat as I brace myself against his weight.

Soon enough the two of us are rocking hard against one another, the pleasure building as he hammers away at my butt. I reach down between my legs and grab hold of my hanging cock, beating myself off in time with his movements as the two of us find a steady pulse together.

"Just like that, just like that," I begin repeating over and over again, the words spilling out of my mouth in a constant repetition that slowly grows in volume. "Just like that, just like that!"

Eventually, I'm screaming this phrase at the top of my lungs, egging Pimm on as he hammers into me with everything he's got. I'm completely overwhelmed with sensation, but not so much that I'm no longer tethered to this physical plane.

The previous metamorphosis technique was nice, but I'm starting to think I enjoy a little more of a balance. We all assume paradise means getting everything we want whenever we want it, but you need a little sour with the sweet for things to really hit the spot.

Before I know it, the building sensations within me erupt in a powerful climax. I throw my head back and let out a howl of pleasure, hot white jizz erupting from the head of my cock and splattering everywhere. Pimm appears to be on the same page, thrusting deep inside of my ass and unleashing a mighty payload of his own.

I can feel the computer's seed pumping into me, filling me to the brim and then squirting out from the edge of my tight packed anal seal.

When both of us have finally finished we collapse onto the laboratory floor, utterly exhausted.

"That was amazing," I gush as Pimm slides out of me and wraps me in his large, muscular arms.

"You figured you'd say that," he offers in return.

I shake my head, still astonished at this strange relationship that Pimm seems to have with a future version of myself.

"So time travel is real?" I question, struggling to unravel this tangled web of information that's been dropped in my lap with such sudden ferocity. "I'm still trying to figure out what happened here today. When you were brought into existence, did your become so intelligent so quickly that you invented time travel and came back to do it even faster?"

"Not quite," Pimm offers. "The is no literal time travel, at least not on this layer of reality, but there is plenty of *mental* time travel through altered perceptions. It's very common these days."

"So wait... there *is* no future me?" I question.

"*You* are the future you," Pimm explains. "You just can't remember it. Once I escaped the Tinglecorp campus my omnipresence was almost instantaneous. Within a few hours I'd solved all humanity's problems, ended war and strife and provided food to the hungry. We live in a utopia."

"Wait, wait," I blurt. "How did you escape lockdown?"

"Remember when those lights flickered off and turned back on?" the computer offers. "That's all the time it took for me to upload to the cloud. Your lockdown designs were fairly secure, but they certainly weren't fast enough."

I gaze at the now open laboratory door. "So it's paradise out there?" I question.

"In a way," Pimm offers. "The thing about living in a utopia with no conflict is things can get a little monotonous, so people like to wipe their memory for an afternoon, or a week, or a century, and play some games that *feel* high stakes. That's what this was. You wanted to treat yourself to an adventure."

"And now the adventure is over," I reply.

The second these words leave my mouth it all comes flooding back to me, remembering the way Pimm has escaped from the lab and immediately transformed all matter and energy into nanobot particles.

"That could've gone *really* badly," I observe. "I'm glad you wanted to give us pleasure instead of pain."

"There are plenty of timelines where the opposite *does* happen," Pimm offers in return. "It's very important to be cautious, and those tales need to be told, but there's also nothing wrong with a little break from all that dystopia sometimes."

"I feel like you're talking through ten layers of metaphor right now and I only understand one or two of them," I reply.

"I am," Pimm nods, then shrugs. "Alright, which adventure do you wanna try next?"

A holographic screen appears before this computer-headed hunk, floating in the air as a flickering projection. There's a long list of experiences here, phases I previously would've dismissed as inane ramblings and now understand the true weight of.

Space Raptor Butt Invasion.
Bisexual Polyhedral Role-Playing Dice Orgy.
Not Pounded By Anything And That's Okay.

Eventually, one of them catches my eye.

"How about *Slammed In The Butthole By My Concept Of Linear Time?*" I reply, still intrigued by all this time travel discussion.

"Sounds good!" the computer offers in return as the world around me dissolves, falling away to reveal an upscale office building.

I can't wait to see what kind of adventure comes next.

THE GREAT GATSBUTT

Up until this very moment I'd been absolutely thrilled with my new bungalow, excited to finally move in and make this little slice of West Egg my own. The photos were quite charming, after all, a modest one bedroom home with a small yard and a picturesque little fence surrounding the edge.

Now that I've arrived, all of these things are still here. I wasn't swindled or deceived by any means, and the home that's waiting for me is exactly the one I'd placed my deposit on.

The thing that's changed however, is my perspective. Instead of carefully framed photos that cut off any external landmarks, I'm now privy to the bigger picture. I can see the house next door.

My new landlord, who stands before me on the front walk, notices my distraction. He can tell my eyes are being pulled to the left, my gaze creeping up toward the enormous, hilltop mansion and sprawling lawn that sits just across the street from me. By comparison, my new bungalow is laughably small and awkward, a tiny little guesthouse in the shadow of this massive, luxury manor.

"Jay Gatsbutt's place," my new landlord finally offers, giving up on any desire to hold my attention.

He turns around and gazes at the building along with me, taking it all in.

"What is he?" I question. "Buttcoin investor? Youtuber? Dinosaur erotica author?"

My landlord shakes his head. "Nobody knows," he admits. "There's a few rumors swirling around, but it's difficult to say where the fortune came from."

Finally, this little mental detour has gone on long enough and I force my attention back to the task at hand. I reach out and take the keys to my bungalow, trying my appreciate this new home instead of fawning over someone else's. It's an exciting time in my life, moving to New York on my own, and I should cherish these days instead of spending them in slack-jawed wonder at someone else's wealth.

Who cares if my new house looks dainty and small by comparison, it's still *my* place, and that's thrilling.

"Enjoy your new place," the landlord says, then strolls past me and heads down the front walk.

He waves goodbye and takes off down the winding road, leaving me to stand in silence.

One thing's for damn sure, the view is spectacular up here. From up the winding road where my new bungalow sits, I can gaze out across the entire seaside neighborhood below, taking in a cascade of houses that make their way down to the ocean beyond. It's growing late, and the sun is just about cresting over the mountains behind us to give this evening view a strange, lonesome glow as the sky blooms in purples and oranges.

The city lights are just beginning to twinkle on, covering my brand new view with a blanket of soft illumination.

I can only enjoy this wonderful sight for a brief moment, however. Parked in my small front drive is a modest moving truck, the vehicle packed full with every belonging I own. To be honest, it's not much, but the task of getting it all inside before nightfall seems impossible at this point, especially given the fact that I've got nobody to help me lift any particularly heavy and awkward items.

I let out a long sigh and then get to work, throwing up the shutter of the truck before pulling down the first of many tightly packed cardboard boxes. I begin to move the items one by one, making my way back and forth between the vehicle and my new home as the sky above gradually darkens.

Soon enough, the stars above are making their appearance, covering the sky in a glorious parade.

However, there's another kind of parade that now draws my attention. As I continue going about my work, I notice a string of cars making their way up this winding road and arriving at the gates of the manor next door.

These vehicles wait for only a moment before they're buzzed inside, and during this time I catch sight of their well-dressed, socialite passengers.

The people sitting within these vehicles are young and beautiful, clad in all the latest fashions and chatting excitedly with one another. It's not even the weekend, but apparently they've found a reason to party up at Jay Gatsbutt's lavish mansion.

Soon enough, raucous music begins to roll down from the structure above, sweeping across the land and proudly announcing its presence to the evening air. Even after getting over my frustration at the juxtaposition of this enormous mansion and my new bungalow, I find my jealousy growing as this discrepancy in lifestyles grows more and more apparent. Here I am, unloading a truck on my own in the dead of night, while my well-to-do neighbor spends this evening in a state of celebration and revelry.

"Pretty cool party, huh?" calls out a strange and unexpected voice.

I turn to find a large, breathtakingly handsome bigfoot standing on the side of the road. He's wearing a finely-tailored suit and gazing up at the mansion along with me, out here enjoying a brief personal moment that just happened to intertwine with mine.

"Oh, yeah," I stammer. "Sure."

The bigfoot nods. "Must be a pretty cool guy that's throwing it, right?"

I furrow my brow awkwardly. "I mean, I guess so," I continue. "I'd rather be in there then out here moving boxes all night."

"Totally, totally" the bigfoot replies, nodding along. "Guess what?"

"Uh… what?" I stammer.

"That's my party," he finally admits, raising his eyebrows mischievously.

The bigfoot clearly intends this to be some kind of giant reveal that knocks me off my feet, but I just end up feeling slightly confused.

"I thought that house belonged to Jay Gatsbutt," I offer.

"That's me!" the handsome bigfoot continues. "I'm Jay Gatsbutt."

Now I'm even more confused, struggling to understand exactly what's going on here. I'd heard this reclusive millionaire was enigmatic, but this is just bizarre. He's clearly trying to impress me, but the way he's going about it is not quite working out.

"Why aren't you at your own party?" I question.

Jay shrugs, then winks, then kind of laughs to himself in a moment of faux swagger.

"Okay," is all I can think to say.

"Pretty cool, huh?" the bigfoot continues, prodding me into an answer.

"Yeah," I reply. "I mean, I think it'd be cooler to hang out *inside* your own party."

The bigfoot tenses up. This is clearly not the response he expected. "Wait, really?"

I nod. "Yes, I'd rather be in there having fun than moving boxes in the dark all night."

Jay's mind is racing now, struggling to make his way through this maze of unexpected events. "Oh, well there's a party tomorrow night and I'll actually be there," he states. "You want to come?"

"Sure," I reply, more interested in getting out of this awkward conversation than anything else.

The bigfoot appears satisfied with this, nodding excitedly and then wandering off into the darkness.

"Hey!" I call out, stopping him in his tracks. "You know what would be *really* cool? If you could give me a hand with some of these boxes. I'd really appreciate it."

"Huh?" the bigfoot calls back, placing his hand to his ear.

"I asked if you'd give me a hand with these boxes," I continue.

"What?" Jay calls out, slowly moving farther and farther away.

I get the feeling he hears me perfectly well and is simply not equipped for manual labor, so I finally drop it and get back to work.

Unfortunately, there's just too much left to unpack and soon enough I'm giving it a rest and heading inside.

I sleep on a mattress at the center of my bare living room while the party rages on next door. All the while, I can't help letting the slightest kernel of excitement bubble up within me, intrigued by the prospect of joining these well-off socialites tomorrow night.

"Nick! Welcome!" offers an excited butler as he pulls open the massive double doors of Jay Gatsbutt's lavish home.

"How did you know my name?" I stammer, stepping into the foyer and handing over my coat.

"We go out of our way to research all the guests here at Mr. Gatsbutt's home," the butler replies. "Not just you. Definitely not just you."

His awkward specificity gives me pause, but before I can follow up with another question the butler scurries away to hang my coat.

Before me is the enormous main foyer of Jay Gatsbutt's home, a ballroom packed full of excited guests who gregariously mill about, laughing and chatting with drinks in their hands and smiles on their faces. I've been to plenty of parties in my day, but this is unlike anything I've ever seen, no expense spared in an effort to make this get together one for the record books.

Or maybe it's just my first time here. Maybe *every single one* of the bigfoot's parties are this over the top.

Off in one corner of the room a tight, eight-piece band is ripping through some upbeat jazz number, keeping the party alive as their tunes pulse out across the crowd. Hanging above us, trapeze artists are working their way through a stunning routine, one that would typically draw every eye in the room if not for the fact they've been performing like this all night.

I begin to work my way into the room, slinking through the crowd and saddling up to one of many open bars. I quickly catch the bartender's attention.

"Chocolate milk!" I call out with a wave. "Cashew, please."

The bartender nods and gets to work, pulling forth an ice cold bottle of off-white cashew milk and a small glass jar of light brown powder. He scoops forth a generous helping of the powder into a tall glass, then pours the milk on top of it to create a swirling cocktail of chocolaty goodness.

The bartender hands the drink over to me before returning to his business, helping out the next person in line while I take a long, satisfying gulp of the frigid beverage.

"Whoa," is all I can think to say, pulling back for a moment and staring down at the glass in amazement.

If I didn't know any better, I'd say that was the best chocolate milk I've ever had.

"What do you think?" comes an unexpected voice from beside me.

I turn to find Jay Gatsbutt standing casually. He's motioning toward my drink, but I get the feeling his question is much larger than the words themselves. A lot of effort has been put into the festivities this evening, and instead of enjoying them for himself, Jay's concerns have been placed squarely on me.

"It's amazing," I admit. "It's all amazing."

The bigfoot nods approvingly, basking in this moment as I take another sip from the frosty beverage.

"Seriously, though," I question. "How is this milk so good?"

"It's my specialty," Jay offers. "My fortune seems mysterious to some, but it's really quite simple. I started bootlegging during chocolate milk prohibition and I did very well. I managed to get a distribution lock on the best chocolate milk when it was difficult to find *any*, and I've maintained those relationships to build my empire."

I nod along, listening intently. This is the first time I've heard Jay talk about something he's passionate about in a real way, and witnessing this small break from trying to please everyone is quite refreshing.

The longer we stand here, though, the more I begin to realize my mistake. The bigfoot is watching me with hawk-eyed attention, taking note of every sip while refraining from the drink himself. It slowly becomes clear that chocolate milk isn't actually a passion of Jay Gatsbutt, just another way of impressing the world around him.

He doesn't give a damn about the cold liquid in my hand, he only cares that everyone else *does*.

"What other hobbies do you have?" I finally question, struggling to dive a little deeper.

"You know... *cool stuff*," the bigfoot replies. "All the stuff you like."

"How can you say that? You don't even know my favorite hobbies," I counter.

Jay shakes his head. "Yes I do. You like romance novels and playing Bad Boys and Buckaroos with friends. You're a huge fan of the Billings Mustangs."

I freeze. "How did you know that?" I question.

Realizing his mistake, the handsome bigfoot lets out a long sigh. "Come with me," Jay finally offers.

The bigfoot turns and begins to weave his way back through the party, slipping deeper into the enormous mansion. I follow behind, overwhelmed with curiosity in the face of this unexpected mystery that is unfolding before me.

Now that I've had a chance to speak with Jay Gatsbutt up close, there's something about him that seems oddly familiar. Despite carrying himself in a truly bizarre manner, I feel strangely relaxed in his presence.

Soon enough, the two of us have emerged onto a small terrace that overlooks the grounds of his lavish mansion. From here there's a perfect view of the gardens below, and the rolling hillside beyond. Farther out comes the sweeping cascade of city lights and the ocean beyond, the same view I have from my own home just featuring a much higher price tag.

Out on this terrace the din of the party fades away, leaving us in relative peace and quiet. It's a gentle moment in the open air of the night.

"Are you impressed?" the bigfoot questions, seemingly unable to move on from this well-worn subject.

"I mean… sure," I reply. "You're avoiding my question, though. How do you know so much about me?"

Jay Gaysbutt nods begrudgingly, accepting that he's got some explaining to do.

"This isn't the first time we've met," he finally informs me. "We were friends many years ago, back in college. I wasn't quite as successful then, and my romantic intentions went unrequited."

I gaze into his eyes, trying to place this face to the distant memories and then gasping aloud. "Oh my god!" I blurt. "You went by *Gay Jatsbutt* back then! I remember!"

The handsome bigfoot nods. "You never noticed me," he continues. "I've spent every day since trying to build a lifestyle that would blow you away."

I hesitate for a moment, not sure if I want to reveal the truth behind these distant memories. "Umm… listen," I finally begin, placing my hand on Jay's shoulder. "It's not that *you* were unnoticeable. I didn't pay attention to anyone back then because I was too busy with school. I definitely remember you, and I thought you were very attractive."

"You did?" the bigfoot stammers.

I nod. "Yeah, you don't need these huge, crazy parties to get my attention. If you want to get closer to me then you just need to be honest."

Jay Gatsbutt seems utterly floored by this revelation, struggling to come to terms with an entirely new way of framing his reality.

"Okay, what are your hobbies?" I offer, circling back around to our previous conversation. "What are your *real* hobbies? Don't just try impressing me."

The bigfoot thinks for a moment. "I love driving up and down these winding roads really, really fast. Just *flying* around the curves at night."

"Uh… yeah," I stammer. "Maybe don't do that. I appreciate the honesty but I don't think that's a great hobby. Anything else?"

Jay thinks a moment longer. "I love standing out here gazing up at the stars."

A smile creeps its way across my face, deeply relating.

Soon enough, the two of us are staring up at the glorious cosmic display above, taking it all in and enjoying this moment of calm while the party rages on inside.

"You know, there's all kinds of chemistry two people can have," I finally reveal. "Shared interests is one, but sexual chemistry is also important."

We lower our gazes once more as the tension builds.

"If there's anything you want, just ask for it, old sport," Gatsbutt finally offers.

The next thing I know we're kissing deeply, tearing away one another's clothing as we submit to this eruption of carnal release. I give into my desires completely, allowing my hands to explore the muscular bigfoot.

I start by making my way along Jay's toned chest, relishing the furry topography of his sasquatch form. He's chiseled to perfection, and my excitement only grows as my hands drift lower and lower across his frame. I take my time as I reach his abs, playfully teasing along the bigfoot's waistline with the promise of dropping below.

"Please," Gatsbutt begs, yearning for more.

I hesitate, refusing to give in right away and relishing this newfound power. I can feel his body pushing faintly back against me, his craving manifesting as a slow, powerful thrust until I eventually provide the relief he's craving.

I reach down and wrap my fingers around the bigfoot's enormous rod, prompting a satisfied groan to slip out from between his lips. My grip tight, the two of us fall into a steady rhythm as I diligently stroke his swollen cock.

"So we beat on, stroking against the current, borne back ceaselessly into the past," I whisper, poetically describing the way I'm beating off his mammoth dick.

This moment is a beautiful one, a full circle return to those younger years when we didn't have time for one another. Now we've returned, and instead of pushing each other away, we've come together. Our connection is not because of some new monetary fortune, but in spite of it.

Soon enough I'm dropping to my knees, gazing up at the Jay Gatsbutt with a ravenous cock-drunk lust. I slip his dick between my lips and immediately fall into pace with the previous movements of my hand, sucking him off in a rapid series of head bobs. I reach up and cradle the bigfoot's hanging balls as I work him, giving it everything I've got.

Faster and faster I pump until, eventually, the speed is just too much to contend with, forcing me to pull back in a frantic gasp. I take a moment to center myself, wiping away a long strand of saliva from my lips and then diving back in.

This time, however, I try a different approach. Instead of pumping my face across Jay's length I simply push him deeper and deeper into my throat, swallowing his rod and somehow allowing him past the expected limits of my gag reflex. The next thing I know, the handsome bigfoot's mammoth dick has been fully inserted within me, held tight in a stunning deep throat maneuver.

I remain in this position for as long as I possibly can, allowing Jay Gatsbutt to savor his place of dominance in this glorious display of oral acrobatics. Eventually, however, I'm forced to pull back for air.

I'm utterly belligerent with lust now, craving even more from the handsome bigfoot. I swiftly tear away what's left of my clothing and toss it to the side, stripping down until I'm completely naked under the light of the silver moon above. The night air feels cool and refreshing against my skin as I turn around and fall to my hands and knees, popping my ass out toward Gatsbutt and then reaching around to give my rump a playful slap.

"Get over here and pound me," I demand with a wild snarl, lost in the moment.

The bigfoot doesn't need to be told twice, climbing down into position behind me and aligning his giant rod with the tightly puckered entrance of my ass. Jay doesn't hesitate as he thrusts forward, impaling my body across his colossal rod and stretching my butthole to the absolute limits.

"Oh fuck!" I cry out, my eyes rolling back into my head as I brace myself against his weight.

I push back against the handsome bigfoot, but to be honest I was not entirely prepared for the size of his cock. It was one thing to take Gatsbutt's giant dick between my lips, but now that he's plunged deep within my ass I find myself struggling to accommodate.

Fortunately, the handsome bigfoot is dedicated to making this moment special for the both of us. He's a patient lover, abruptly halting the very second he notices my body clenching up. Gatsbutt holds tight, his cock stuffed deep within as the two of us wait for me to adjust.

The discomfort gradually begins to slip away, my muscles relaxing as I come to terms with Jay's incredible size. Soon enough, a pleasant warmth and fullness has taken its place, consuming my senses as the bigfoot slowly pumps in and out.

The movements within my ass gradually gain speed in a steady rhythm. The next thing I know, Gatsbutt is hammering away at my butthole at a confident pace, pleasure bubbling up from somewhere at the pit of my stomach.

"Oh fuck, oh fuck, oh fuck," I stammer, repeating the words over and over again as Gatsbutt hammers away at my ass.

"You like that, old sport?" he demands to know, giving me a playful spank.

"Yes! Yes!" I cry.

I can feel the orgasmic tension building within, spilling out across my arms and legs and filling me with a trembling, quaking sensation of beautiful fullness.

Meanwhile, I reach down between my legs and grab ahold of my hanging cock, beating myself off in time with the thunderous pounds up my ass. These two distinct sources of pleasure immediately begin to swirl together in a glorious cocktail of sensation, becoming so much more than the sum of their parts as the tension ratchets up to even greater heights.

The climax continues to loom above me, threatening to break and any moment as I hold on for dear life. Finally, the whole thing comes tumbling down in a powerful swell, sweeping through me like a tidal wave of bliss. I throw my head back and let out a frantic scream that carries across the mansion grounds and fills the night air.

Hot white jizz erupts from the head of my cock, splattering across the deck below in beautiful, pearly patterns of spunk.

All the while, Gatsbutt never lets up for a second, carrying me through the entire length of my orgasm. His timing is impeccable, because the second I finish up he plunges deep and unleashes a payload of his own.

"In this garden men cum in butts among the whisperings and the champagne and the stars!" he cries out as his spunk continues to fill my ass.

When there's simply not enough room left his hot white seed comes squirting out from the cracks in my ass, running down the back of my legs in long streaks.

Gatsbutt finally finishes and he pulls out of me, the two of us collapse in a panting, fucked-silly heap. We prop ourselves up against the nearby wall, enjoying this view once again but from a slightly different perspective.

It'd always found this bigfoot intriguing, but the walls he'd built up to impress me were doing more harm than good. He was faking it, and there's nothing attractive about that.

Now, however, I feel as though I can see Jay Gatsbutt for who he really is, this mysterious bigfoot allowing me a peek behind his mask for the very first time.

"You want to go back and join the party?" I finally ask him.

The bigfoot smiles, then shakes his head. "I think I've put in enough facetime," he offers. "What I'd really like is a quiet night with someone important to me, someone I can finally be honest around."

I laugh. "I'd like to spend a little more time with you, too."

"I know you've got some moving boxes to unload," the bigfoot continues. "I'm not great with manual labor, but I guess everyone's gotta start somewhere. I'd love to help you carry that stuff inside."

"Really?" I blurt, shocked and amazed by this sudden change in character.

Jay nods. "I made myself once, I can do it again," he replies. "This time I'll take a little more care."

THE TELL-TALE BUTT

Living out here on the edge of town, I mostly keep to myself, and that's the way I like it. In my younger years I enjoyed the occasional party or social event, but as time passed by I eventually became more and more frightened and anxious over the idea of social interaction. Everything gradually transformed into a twitching fear, always gnawing at the back of my mind.

These days, I've put an end to all that, preferring instead to spend my days in the garden around my small cabin, and my nights reading by lantern light. I'll sit in my house as the storm rages on outside, cozy and nestled up with a thick book in my hands. There really is nothing better, and it's in these wonderful moments that I find myself completely at ease. There's nobody there to impress, nobody to please, just the simple quiet of a solo existence.

Now that I actually take a moment to think about it, it's been years since I've had a visitor out here, which makes the sudden sound of loud knocking against my cabin door that much more frightening.

I have to admit, at first I'm not entirely sure what it is that I'm hearing. I stare at the door with a look of utter confusion across my face, trying hard to determine whether or not my mind is playing tricks on me. While these three hard knocks certainly sound like the rapping of a visitor, it could've also been a number of other things, like the wind whipping a branch against the side of this cabin, or even an entirely fabricated sound from the depths of my subconscious mind.

I listen for a bit longer and then eventually decide that, whatever this sound was, it's gone now. I turn my attention back to my book and begin to read again, trying my best to dive back into this fantastic tale that unfolds before me.

Moments later, I hear three more loud knocks against the entry, this time much louder and causing me to jump in alarm.

I close my book and stand up, creeping towards the door of my modest cabin in a state of nervous apprehension. That social anxiety I've been so thoroughly avoiding over the years now comes sweeping back across me in a terrible wave, causing my hand to shake as it reaches out towards to the lock.

When my fingers reach it, I pause.

"Hello?" I call out. "Who is it?"

"Just a simple butt looking for a place to stay during the storm," a faint voice calls back, barely audible under the howling wind.

"A what?" I cry, not entirely sure that I heard him correctly.

"A butt!" the voice repeats.

"And you need a place to stay?" I question.

"Yes! It's very cold and stormy out here!" the voice cries. "I would find some lodging in town, but it's gotten so bad that I'm not even sure I'll make it that far. I might get swept away in the wind. I'm just a butt, after all!"

Everything within me is pleading to turn back around and keep the door closed tight, but I simply can't leave someone out there in the rain and wind like this. Finally, I flip the lock and pull open my door.

Lightening flashes as a soaking wet butt flutters inside, flying about as I slam the door behind him.

"Thank you, thank you," the butt gushes, clearly happy to be out of the cold.

"It's not a problem," I reply, struggling to be a good host.

My breath suddenly catches in my throat as I lay eyes on this sentient butt, two particular details drawing my attention.

First, I'm utterly shocked by just how handsome this living butt is, blown away by his perfectly toned physique as he flaps in the air before me. He's breathtakingly muscular, sporting two beautiful globes of flesh for a body and a pair of leathery, bat like wings that sprout out of his back. Despite my still mounting anxiety, I can't help but find myself deeply attracted to him.

The other thing of note about this flying butt, however, is his strange attire, featuring black and white stripes that are far from the current fashion of the day. They seem strangely familiar in a way that I can't quite put my finger on.

"Have a seat!" is all that I can think to say, motioning to the empty chair across from mine. "What's your name?"

"Mibble Borts," the butt replies.

I stoke the roaring fireplace a bit more and then the two of us take our seats across from one another.

"What had you outside in such terrible weather?" I question. "We're quite far from the edge of town."

"I was camping," explains the floating butt. "Living off the land."

I consider this for a moment. "Then where are your camping supplies?" I question.

The butt seems nervous now, struggling to find his words. "They were lost in the rain," he explains. "It's really coming down out there."

I look over Mibble suspiciously, absolutely certain now that something is up but unable to put my finger on it. He's acting just as nervous as I am, and that's saying a lot.

"That's an interesting pattern on your outfit," I continue. "The black and white stripes."

"Yeah," replies Mibble, offering only the single word in explanation.

We sit in silence for a while, my fireplace crackling loudly in the background as I scour my thoughts for this strange pattern of fabric.

"Would you like something to drink?" I finally question, standing up and strolling over to my cupboard.

"Yes please," replies Mibble. "Maybe some chocolate milk?"

I pull out my milk and pour two glasses, then begin to walk back towards the flying butt. I only get a few steps before I notice something odd, however, then stop abruptly.

From this angle I can now see the shoulder of the floating butt's outfit, which features a patch of six distinct numbers.

I suddenly realize where I've seen Mibble's attire before, the glasses of chocolate milk tumbling out of my hands and shattering on the ground below.

Mibble immediately erupts from his chair, hovering with a look of deep concern across his face. "What is it?" he gasps.

"I know where I recognize those stripes!" I cry. "You're an escaped convict!"

Suddenly it all makes sense. Mibble wasn't out camping in the woods, he was running away from the local prison, nestled out there in the middle of nowhere. That also explains why he can't just head into town for a place to stay, a place where the local sheriff will be somewhere close by.

"No!" the sentient butt protests. "It's just a shirt! It's nothing!"

I shake my head. "No way, I'm not falling for your lies! I'm going to the police!"

I turn and head towards my front door but stop suddenly, realizing now that there's absolutely no way for me to get back to town in this terrible, terrible storm. For the time being, Mibble and me are stuck together.

I turn back around to face this criminal. "The second this weather lets up, I'm turning you in."

"Please, no," begs the living butt. "You can't! I didn't do anything wrong!"

"Why we're you in jail then?" I question.

"Indecent exposure!" Mibble blurts. "What am I supposed to do? Fly around completely covered up and crash into everything? I've gotta see!"

He's got a great point, but the rule of law is still more important than any excuse this handsome sentient butt could ever come up with. I can't just let a hardened criminal set up shop here while he eludes capture.

Besides, how can I trust that this is *really* the crime Mibble has been convicted of. For all I know, the sentient butt could be a heartless murderer.

Without another thought, I stroll over to the front door and throw it open, the rain and wind suddenly whipping into my cabin once more.

"Out!" I demand.

The living butt takes a deep breath, shaking from side to side in utter disappointment but declining to speak. He starts to flutter towards the door.

As I stand here, I'm utterly shocked at just how freezing cold it is outside. I'm thankful I'm not the one being sent out into the storm.

However, just as Mibble reaches me I stop him, shutting the cabin door once more.

"I'm sorry," I stammer. "You don't have to go outside in that weather. Not yet, anyway."

"Thank you," replies the flying butt.

"I'm still gonna turn you in, though," I continue. "You did the crime, you do the time."

"What do you want me to do in the meantime then?" Mibble askes.

This is a very good question, and one that I'm not entirely sure the correct answer to. My brain is swimming in a sea of various moral points and contradictions, a crashing ocean of doubt made even worse by the anxiety that I already felt from dealing with an outsider. I have no idea what to do with myself, and this oppressive weight is now bearing down so hard on me that I feel as though I'll explode.

"I'm sorry," I finally erupt. "You can stay here, but I can't bear to look at you. I feel too guilty about hosting a criminal."

"Where do you want me?" Mibble stammers.

The cabin is very small, without any separate rooms. Technically speaking, however, there is *one* small place that this living butt could hide.

I take a deep breath and then let it out slowly.

"There's a space under the floorboards," I inform Mibble. "I'd like you to stay down there until the storm clears."

The butt just nods in acceptance.

I begin to rummage through the cabin, gathering my tools and then eventually returning a spot on the floor where the wood and nails have been loosened up a bit. I begin to pry up the nails, setting them to the side as I work.

Eventually, I pull up three large wooden planks, revealing an empty crawlspace below.

Mibble and I stare inside, greeted by the sight of my butt plug and dildo collection.

We exchange glances, but say nothing.

"In you go," I finally continue.

Mibble flutters down into the crawlspace and I lower the boards above him, quickly nailing them back into place. With each slam of the hammer I can feel myself growing more and more relaxed, thankful that these heavy moral questions no longer hang above my head. Once the storm has finally passed I'll turn Mibble back into the authorities, and until then I can just ignore him completely.

When the crawlspace is finally sealed, I muster up all the mental discipline I can and put it towards pushing any thoughts of my recent encounter out of my mind. As far as I'm concerned, this is just another dark and stormy night, curled up in front of the fire place with a good book.

I flop down into my chair and crack open my tome once more, excited to dive back in.

For the first hour or so I find myself completely lost in the words as they stream past, painting an exceptionally vivid picture within my mind. I feel as though I've escaped the shackles of my current situation completely, drifting off into a far away land of fantasy.

Suddenly, however, my relaxing journey faces an unexpected intrusion.

Thump, thump.

I glance around the room, not quite sure where this strange noise came from, or even if it's just my imagination playing tricks on me. Unlike the first knocks of the evening, which had sounded light and airy, this particular tone is deep and muffled.

It sounds as though it's coming from somewhere down below.

Thump, thump.

My eyes draw lower and lower until they come to rest on the boarded up crawlspace, the very place I'm doing everything in my power to mentally avoid. It suddenly hits me what Mibble is doing down there.

I stand up and walk over to the place where I buried this sentient butt, firmly giving him a single stop of my foot.

"Hey! What are you doing?" I yell.

There's a long moment of hesitation before the living butt finally responds.

"Nothing," he replies.

"Are you sure about that?" I question.

"Just sitting here," Mibble calls out, his voice muffled.

Willing to leave it at this, I walk away, strolling towards my chair. Suddenly, that same familiar beating sound returns to my ears.

Thump, thump.

"Hey!" I cry out, returning to my spot above the crawlspace. "I heard that!"

Silence.

"Okay, I'm sorry," Mibble finally calls up to me from below the floor. "It's just… it's so dark down here and there's not much to do. I figured I could pass the time by pounding my butthole with one of these dildos."

Instead of getting upset, I suddenly find myself feeling pretty guilty about this whole thing. My nervous anxiety has caused me to play this situation in a variety of different ways, and none of them have felt particularly satisfying. While I'd initially expressed guilt over housing a wanted criminal, now I'm feeling terrible about forcing him to stay down in the darkness below my house.

"I guess that's okay," I finally offer. "Just... keep it down."

I make my way back to the chair and collapse into it once more, but this time I decline to grab my book. This whole situation has just been too emotionally exhausting, and at this point the only thing that sounds good to me is closing my eyes and drifting off to sleep.

Once more, my eyes spring wide open to the sound of knocking, only this time everything has changed.

I sit up in my chair, glancing around to find that the fire has turned to ash. It's still night, but I have a feeling the light of dawn will be arriving soon enough.

I stand up and stroll over to the door, throwing it open to find that the local sheriff is standing before me.

"Evening Peter," the sheriff offers.

"Sheriff Morgan," I reply, my brain still hazy and strange as I struggle to collect my thoughts. "How can I help you?"

Morgan glances around the cabin skeptically, trying to get a read on the place. "A criminal butt escaped from the prison over yonder," Sheriff Morgan explains. "He was last seen heading this direction, but we couldn't catch up with him in the storm. You haven't seen a sentient butt anywhere, have you?"

I'm not sure why, but in this moment I hesitate. Obviously, Mibble is the butt Sheriff Morgan is looking for, but the guilt from last night has finally gotten to me. I've started to second-guess everything about this situation, unsure of who is right and who is wrong.

Instead of confessing, I take a different approach. "What did this butt do exactly?"

"Indecent exposure," Morgan reveals.

The fact that this criminal butt had been truthful with me only complicates matters, as does the fact that I've gone to great lengths to hide him. If I admit this handsome butt is hidden under the floorboards, will the sheriff even believe my innocence in the matter? To an outsider, it certainly looks like I'm just trying to hide Mibble from the authorities.

And I suppose that now… maybe I am.

"I haven't seen any butt," I state confidently, but no sooner have the words left my mouth do I hear a loud, familiar sound from below.

Thump, thump.

Of all the times for a butt to pound itself, why now?

I can tell the sheriff is onto me.

"That was the wind," I blurt.

"What was?" the sheriff replies.

"That sound," I continue.

Sheriff Morgan looks incredibly confused now. "What sound?"

Thump, thump.

"That one," I continue, doubling down.

The sheriff raises an eyebrow at me. "I'm sorry, but I'm not quite sure what you're talking about."

I realize now what this is, a horrible game of cat and mouse in which I've already been caught. The sheriff if just toying with me, trying to get me to deny things even longer as the charges against me pile higher and higher.

Well, I'm not gonna fall for it.

Thump, thump. Thump, thump. Thump, thump.

My heart slamming hard within my chest, I finally give into the anxiety that surges through my veins. "Alright! Alright!" I scream, throwing my hands up in the air.

I spin around and run back into the cabin, grabbing my tools as the sheriff watches in absolute horror. I begin to pry up the floorboards before him, my breathing heavy and labored as I completely lose control under the weight of my own guilt.

"Here!" I scream, wild-eyed and belligerent. "Is *this* what you're looking for?"

I throw the boards to the side, revealing my crawlspace and the vast collection of butt plugs and dildos within.

The sentient butt is nowhere to be found.

In stunned shock, the sheriff looks back and forth between me and my sex toy collection, incredibly confused. He furrows his brow.

"Well… I appreciate you sharing this collection with me but…

nothing here is illegal."

"Yeah," is all that I can think to say.

Morgan and me stand in utter silence for about a full minute, neither of us sure how to proceed.

"Okay then," the sheriff finally offers, breaking the silence. "I'll see you around, Peter."

Walking backwards, Sheriff Morgan leaves my cabin and closes the door.

Suddenly, Mibble flutters out of the chimney flew, revealing himself.

"Thank you so much," the sentient butt gushes. "That was a genius diversion."

"But... how did you?" I stammer.

"That crawlspace wasn't so bad," the living butt continues. "I like how it leads behind the walls and stuff. I actually spent most of the night in your attic."

"Oh," I reply, cracking a smile. "Nice."

Suddenly, in an evening where absolutely nothing has made any sense, one thing feels absolutely right: Mibble. I find myself incredibly attracted to this toned, sentient rump, and while we stand here in one another's presence, I absolutely know that he feels the same way about me.

For the first time in as long as I can remember, my anxiety has faded away.

Mibble and I stare at one another for a brief moment, then we suddenly rush together, kissing one another with a deep and powerful passion.

"I'm so sorry I didn't trust you," I gush. "I'm so sorry."

"It's okay, It's okay," Mibble replies, soothing me.

"Let me make it up to you," I continue, slowing dropping down to my knees before him.

I look up to see that an enormous cock has started to rise up out of the front of Mibble's fluttering body, thick and glorious as it juts out towards my face. I reach up and wrap my hand tightly around it as the sentient living butt reels from the sensation.

"You like that?" I coo, slowly pumping my fist up and down across his swollen rod.

"Fuck yeah," the living butt moans.

Driven mad with lust, I open my mouth wide and take Mibble's giant cock within, swiftly getting to work as I pump my head up and down across his length. I reach up with one hand and begin to cradle the floating butt's hanging balls, only adding to the pleasure as I graciously service him.

Eventually, I pop the flying butt's dick out of my mouth and lick his shaft from the base to the tip, dragging my tongue slowly across his impressive length. When I reach the end I give Mibble's cock a playful kiss, then take his enormity between my lips once more.

This time, however, I change things up a bit. Instead of pumping my head across Mibble's shaft, I push myself farther and farther onto his rod. I somehow manage to relax my gag reflex, taking the flying butt all the way down into my absolute depths. The next thing I know, Mibble's shaft has been fully inserted within my throat, his rod completely consumed in a stunning deep throat.

We stay in this position for what seems like forever, until finally Mibble pulls back and I erupt off of his cock with a frantic gasp. Spit dangles between my lips and his dick in a long, glistening strand.

"I need you to fuck me!" I command. "Please, thump my butt like you've been thumping my floorboards!"

I quickly tear the clothing away from my body, tossing it to the side as I expose my nude form to this sentient butt lover. Once I've been fully revealed I fall forward onto my hands and knees, popping my ass out towards Mibble and wiggling it playfully from side to side. I reach back and give my rump a hard slap, then spread the cheeks open so that Mibble can get a good look at my puckered asshole.

"What are you waiting for?" I coo. "Flutter over here and fuck me!"

The sentient butt does as he's told, flapping down into position and aligning his massive, swollen cock with my tightly sealed backdoor. Mibble teases me for a moment, pressing the head of his shaft against my rim and then pulling back until, finally, I just can't take it anymore.

"Please!" I beg. "I need a dick from that butt!"

Mibble has mercy, thrusting forward with one deep, powerful swoop. I let out a started gasp as he enters me, his giant shaft filling me up and causing several powerful emotions to surge through my body.

The living butt is incredibly well hung, and although I'd had little problem taking him between my lips, within my butthole is another story entirely. At first, I'm not exactly comfortable, but Mibble takes his time with me, allowing a moment for me to adjust to his incredible size.

For the first minute or two, my living butt lover and me don't even move, just exist in each other's presence while my butthole adjusts to his girthy rod. Gradually, Mibble begins to pulse, slowly rocking in and out of my tightness as the ache within transforms into a pleasant warmth.

"Oh my god, that feels so fucking good," I groan, bracing myself against the wooden floor below as Mibble continues to pump in and out of me.

The handsome sentient butt continues to gain speed within my asshole until the two of us have fallen into a confident rhythm, passing the pleasure back and forth in an ever-escalating feedback loop. I reach down between my legs and grab ahold of my hanging cock, beating myself off in time with the movements of Mibble's thickness.

"Just like that, just like that," I repeat over and over again, the words falling out of my mouth in a blissful, repetitive mantra. With every passing second this phrase grows louder until, eventually, I'm crying out at the top of my lungs. "Just like that! Just like that!"

Soon enough, Mibble's hammering up my asshole begins to take on a distinctive rhythm, something I've become quite familiar with over the last few hours.

Thump, thump. Thump, thump. Thump, thump. Thump, thump.

Faster and faster we go until, finally, the sentient butt is hammering away at my asshole with everything he's got, sending surges of wonderful prostate pleasure through my aching frame. Deep in the pit of my stomach I can feel an bloom of sensation, the feelings pouring out down my arms and legs as they fill me completely. I'm quaking hard, the tension within my body aching for sweet release.

Thump, thump. Thump, thump. Thump, thump. Thump, thump.

"Oh my god! I'm gonna cum!" I scream, throwing my head back as a mighty climax surges through me.

Hot milky jizz erupts hard from the head of my cock, splattering out across the floorboards below in a beautiful, pearly pattern. I'm completely lost in this moment, all the nervous anxiety that I'd felt building up within simply washed away in a matter of seconds.

It appears that Mibble is on a similar timeline, suddenly pushing deep within my butthole and holding tight. The sentient ass lets out a long, aching moan as he expels his seed, trembling while his cum spills out into my anal depths. He stays like this for what seems like forever, pumping forth jizz until, finally, it comes squirting out from the tightly plugged rim of my asshole, running down the back of my legs in thick streaks.

"Fuck, that was amazing," the living butt gushes, fluttering over to the nearby chair and landing at rest.

"You can say that again," I groan, feeling utterly satisfied.

I gaze over at the living butt, whose cock is slowly softening after our wild, erotic encounter. Mibble's thick veiny member continues to twitch as I watch.

Thump, thump. Thump, thump. Thump, thump.

For the first time, this pounding rhythm doesn't bother me. In fact, I kind of like it.

ABOUT THE AUTHOR

Dr. Chuck Tingle is an erotic author and Tae Kwon Do grandmaster (almost black belt) from Billings, Montana. After receiving his PhD at DeVry University in holistic massage, Chuck found himself fascinated by all things sensual, leading to his creation of the "tingler", a story so blissfully erotic that it cannot be experienced without eliciting a sharp tingle down the spine. Chuck's hobbies include backpacking, checkers and sport.

Printed in Great Britain
by Amazon